# WHEN WILL PAPA GET HOME?

A STORY OF HOPE

LARADA HORNER-MILLER

HORNER PUBLISHING COMPANY

To buy books in quantity for corporate use or incentives, call **(505) 323-7098** or e-mail <u>**larada@earthlink.net**</u>

This book is a work of fiction. Any references to historical events, real people or real places are used fictitiously. Other characters come from the author's imagination and if they resemble anyone, it is pure coincidence.

Library of Congress Control Number: **2015918403**

**Horner Publishing Company, Tijeras, NM**

ISBN: 0-9966144-0-0

ISBN-13: 978-0-9966144-0-5

❀ Created with Vellum

## DEDICATION

*I dedicate this book to all the storytellers that filled my life with rich and wonderful stories over the years. I had a list prepared to print but was afraid of leaving someone off. So storytellers, you know who you are!*

## ACKNOWLEDGMENTS

A big thank you goes out to the following people:

- Jackie Mock & Rose Ward for telling me how Rose's family moved to the Branson-Trinchera area
- Darien Brown for describing how roofs were made in homesteads
- Joan Doherty for allowing me to go the Philly Place to photograph what remains of the homestead
- Harold Horner for our wonderful time looking around the Philly Place
- My beta-readers for their comments and help: Lin Miller & Sherry McCarty

Research

Richard Louden , *The Branson Story*, (Pueblo: Schusters'

Printing, 1999)

Morris Taylor, *Trinidad, Colorado Territory,* (TSJC, 1966)

Homestead Acts

https://en.wikipedia.orgwikiHomestead_Acts#

Homesteading_requirements

Sections

https://en.wikipedia.org/wiki/Section_(United_States_land_surveying)

Detailed Map of Mexico

http://usa-atlas.com/map1484962_0_0.htm

Pancho Villa

http://www.biography.com/people/pancho-villa-9518733

# PREFACE

My childhood in southeastern Colorado in a small ranching community overflowed with stories. The storytellers told and retold these community stories at a variety of get-togethers: around the Horner round table in our dining room after one of Mom's delicious home-cooked meals, around the fire at the annual branding on our ranch, and around a group of cowboys gathered at a dance or social affair anytime.

One story I loved was about the Philly Place, my favorite spot on our family ranch. It was the story of a Mexican homesteader who was thrown in jail for stealing cattle. My Granddad bought Philly's homestead when he was in jail for this crime. I heard this story often when my Dad and other storytellers gathered and swapped their familiar tales.

When I was in my early thirties, I was home during the summer. My Dad, Mom, and I were out on the ranch, exploring like so many times before. We decided to run by the Philly Place. The old rock walls of the homestead were all that stood. Some of the support beams for the roof, the *vigas*, still laid across the top of the house. The two rooms were identifiable. One was an all-purpose kitchen and living room. An old fainting couch rested in the second room that we assumed was a bedroom.

We had explored enough, and it was time to leave. As I was walking out the front door, I hesitated and looked down. I spied a blue marble lying between the front door and the front step.

I asked my Dad about its owner. He had no idea whose it was, but that marble started wheels turning for me. To whom did the marble belong? I knew the Philly story, so this story evolved from that familiar tale I had heard my whole life and that blue marble.

My imagination added to it, and the story grew. The cow thief became a horse thief, and here it is! Any names mentioned in this story are not real except for the Horner names. I had to add my Granddad and Dad to my story because I heard this tale from them, and my Mom for her famous hugs and hospitality.

# 1

F riday night and my workweek is over. A long awaited "night out with the girls" was my plan for the evening. Rummaging through my jewelry box, I search for my diamond stud earrings, and a childhood treasure catches my eye--a blue marble. Does it seem strange to find a marble in an adult woman's jewelry box? Not to me.

I collapse on my favorite soft velveteen chair exhausted from my busy workweek. Without hesitation, I am back there, at our old rock and adobe homestead house known as "The Philly Place," named after my Papa, Philadelphia Gonzales. The house is located a few miles east of Branson in southeastern Colorado. Many years ago when Papa and Mama first came to the United States from Mexico, his friends nicknamed him "Philly", and it stuck. I am transported back to that little girl sitting on the front steps in my faded flour sack dress playing with this marble in the dirt. I am waiting-- waiting for Papa to get home. The year is 1928.

The rush of feelings and emotions from the past paralyzes me today in that comfortable velveteen chair. Though I'm mentally in 1928, my body is right here in Denver, Colorado at the end of a long work-week in 1960—those precious memories! I hadn't thought of that old place for years. Home--my roots-- my past! Today, I live in Denver, miles away from that homestead. Years have passed. I am away from that life, yet that marble draws me back there again.

Look at me now. I am a forty-year-old international business consultant, divorced with three children, and successful. This country girl matured and became the woman I am today. I allow myself this traipses down memory lane so seldom any more.

For many years, I have put aside a request from Papa. Over the years, it nagged at me often, but I focused on raising my three children as a single Mom and pursuing a career I love. My children have grown: all three are in their twenties, in college and doing well on their own. This blue marble lures me back in time. I don't want to go there--I have plans for the evening. I want an evening with laughter and relaxation with my girlfriends out on the town.

Today, I have all the luxuries of this modern life--hot and cold running water, inside toilet, and a warm solid house. I've forgotten how much I take for granted in this sophisticated world. It is nothing like that drafty rock house where I lived as a child whose only water supply was the nearby creek and reservoir. Our toilet was an outhouse.

The marble rolls around in my smooth well-manicured hand. I lounge back on my soft, velvety chair, lost in the present and its problems. The rush and hurry of my life builds up stress. I compare this peek back into a much more leisurely time to my hectic life today. I yearn for that carefree time of yesterday.

With the help of that blue marble, I'm swept up in a time machine of memories. I am no longer a forty-year-old woman but an eight-year-old child, moved back to one moment in my life that changed my world completely--waiting, waiting, waiting--

"When will Papa get home? *¿Cuándo regresa mi Papa a mi casa?* Huh, Mama, when? *¿Cuándo?*" I dart each question at her as I sit impatiently on the step facing the northeast, with nothing but the vast open prairie for miles--my front yard.

Days drag on when he is away. I miss him so, but he just left two days ago, and he's to be gone for at least a week--oh no! TWO DAYS--what an eternity!

As I sit thinking and waiting on the step, the blue marble turns round and round in my dusty hand. The smooth surface catches on my rough, calloused fingers. I don't have many toys, just my dolly and a few marbles—a newly acquired toy. My favorite marble is the blue one that matches the color of the sky.

"¡Maria, *ven aquí*!" Oh, no! Why does Mama want me to come inside now? What does she want? She's been so restless this time with Papa gone. He goes to Trinidad at least every other month, but this time she's upset about something—I can feel it. There's an edge in her voice. I have seen her wiping her eyes but she stops as soon as I see her. This morning she yelled at me for nothing at all. She usually doesn't yell at me--or at least not like this morning.

She always wants me to help with the household chores:  wash the dishes and sprinkle, tap down and sweep the hard dirt floor, wash the clothes on the scrub board down at the creek. Wash, wash, wash—the list goes on forever! I hate these chores--they're woman's work.

I'd much rather be outside with Papa. I help him

feed the horses and milk the cow. I ride alongside of Papa looking for stray calves or hunting coyotes. All this outside work allows me to be with Papa and be his little helper. His nickname for me is "Shorty," and I love the sound of that name. He's the only one who calls me that.

I don't like housework, but I do love our house--this beautiful, spacious two-room rock and adobe house we built ourselves. At first it was so drafty you could see between the rocks, but the adobe sealed it so it is snug in the winter cold, and cool in the summer heat. It is much better than the lean-to we lived in for two years. I shiver thinking about camping outside in the winter and summer on our travel here from New Mexico.

I was born in Laredo, TX in 1920 so I wasn't around for the long trip from Mexico, but I love to listen to Papa's stories about the trip. It sounded like quite an adventure—I'm sure that I would have enjoyed camping out under the stars but then I remember our trip from New Mexico and it was a shorter trip, so would I have really enjoyed the longer trip from Mexico? I wonder.

Two days are over with Papa gone--how will I survive another?

## 2

A s soon as Papa arrived in the United States from Mexico, he filed a declaration of intention to become a citizen. Many of our friends that came to America before us passed on information to Papa about the importance of doing this. Papa couldn't write, but information was passed around our small community of Nuevo Laredo, Mexico. I had no idea what all this was, but I knew it was important. Papa and Mama talked a lot about it, and they worked hard to get it. In 1926 Papa and Mama gained citizenship while we were living in Branson, CO, and we all celebrated their accomplishment.

I was an American citizen by birth, which really seemed strange because I don't speak any English, only Spanish, and in my heart I am a Mexican. How does that work?

Now that Papa and Mama were United States citizens, they were able to acquire a homestead in Colorado. Our homestead included a quarter section of land--160 acres. To get our new home, we had to live on the homestead for five years. Acquiring the homestead was a three-step process: first, Papa filed a signed application. Second, we would get the land if we improved it by building a house or something Papa called "containments" on it. I didn't know what that meant, but Papa translated it to me to mean walls, fences, roads, paths or gates. It took a couple years before we built the house.

First, we built a lean-to to live in, and then we added a small enclosure for our horses and our small herd of cattle. Our animals took precedence over our house. Papa said the corrals were containments too--oh, the English language. The third step of homesteading was Papa filing a deed for our property. We lived there for five years, so it was ours, truly a dream come true for our little Mexican family.

When we were living in the lean-to, I made friends with a horny toad. I had never seen one before. His spiky body fascinated me. He looked like a miniature dinosaur. When he visited, he explored everything he could. Papa and I played with him and fed him, but Mama didn't like him. We named him Paco.

After that we looked for Paco every morning. At first he didn't come by every day, but we continued feeding and playing with him, so his visits became more routine. He got comfortable enough with me to let me pick him up and hold him in my hand—he just fit in the palm of my small hand, and his scaly body felt sharp and bumpy. He amazed me so much because he looked like a mean creature with his spiked ridges on his sides, but he wasn't at all.

Our next building was an outhouse a few feet away from where Papa planned to build the house. He experimented on it and built it out of sandstone rock from the mesa and adobe mortar to seal the rocks. He liked the results. Later he used the same material to build our home. The big job for the outhouse was digging a deep hole for all the sewage to go into. Papa spent several days working on it, and he sweat a lot. It was hard work. I tried to help, but it seemed I got in the way more than helped.

I loved that outhouse with its seat to sit on. I had never mastered the art of squatting. With my long skirt, it was so hard to not pee all over the hem of my skirt and shoes. Mama loved it too; it didn't matter to

Papa one way or the other, so I think he built it for us two females.

I can't believe the three of us built our house. It is so beautiful. Papa and Mama were used to homes made of adobe bricks, but with all the amazing sandstone rocks in the canyon around us, Papa's experiment on the outhouse worked, so he decided to make our house out of rocks and adobe. He had admired houses in Mora, New Mexico built out of rock and thought they were beautiful. He talked to men there about how to build one, so he was excited to be able to actually have his own rock and adobe house.

During the early spring, we carried the heavy rocks down from the rim rock across the canyon-- about a half-mile south. We tied the rocks to our two horses and drug them to our house site. It was back-breaking work. Then we mixed mud from the river for the adobe mortar. I liked that part the best because it was like making mud pies, but Mama didn't because I stayed muddy and smelly for days. Papa mixed straw and manure into this muddy mixture. "My secret ingredients to make it strong," he chuckled!

The adobe sealed the rocks and made it snug and warm in the winter and cool in the summer.

Mama complained about the smell when we were working, but I didn't notice it. I remember when the stone wall was only as high as my knees. Then when it seemed like magic that Papa put a little square in the wall and it became a window and a big square became a door. We had one window in the kitchen and two in Papa and Mama's bedroom.

I loved the view out the kitchen window facing north and east. I could see Mesa de Mayo and the great open plains. I could see forever.

Papa noticed that many of the residents in Mora, New Mexico had painted the door frame and doors of their houses light blue. After he got acquainted with the people there, he asked the reason for the blue doors. Many friends told him, "For safety! It keeps out the bad spirits."

So on one of Papa's trips to Trinidad before we finished the house, he came back with just enough light blue paint. Papa and I painted the door and what fun we had! We ended up with as much paint on us as on the door and door frame. Mama wrinkled her nose and shook her head. She questioned him about this tradition at first but later grew to love it, especially when our neighbor's wife, Rosa, commented on how nice it looked.

Next we mixed more adobe and plastered the

inside walls to give a smooth even texture—the straw stuck out here and there, so it never was completely smooth, but it made wonderful patterns.

Finally we put on the roof. First we added the *vigas*, large, heavy support wooden beams we drug down from the mesa south of our homestead. The *vigas* span across the house, then we added *ladrillas*, smaller branches that crossed the *vigas*, then brush and dirt. Then we added the adobe mortar to tie it all together. When the roof was complete, we moved inside. That was a day of celebration because now we could sleep inside, out of the elements.

When we moved into our new house, I wondered if Paco would find us or if Mama would let him in. Early the second morning when I opened the door to go outside, Paco sat sunning himself on our front step.

I scooped him up in my skirt and took him with me to the ridge of the arroyo and he sat with me while I watched the sunrise and the scene before me come to life. Deer sauntered across the arroyo to drink. Long eared jack rabbits hopped around them, darting between bushes. A coyote skirted us, wary of getting shot. Paco just sat, observing our world.

A little later, Papa came from the corral and joined us. He burst out laughing when he saw Paco.

"Has this become a trio?" Papa whispered so he didn't disturb our wild guests. I nodded my head with a grin. The three of us enjoyed this ritual many days.

"When will Papa be home? *¿Cuándo regresa mi Papa a mi casa?*" This has been the longest day yet.

## 3

My thoughts move me to look at my hands--calloused and blisters that show the world that I work hard. In fact I had never noticed the condition of my hands until I went to Trinidad with Papa a month ago, and the other children had teased me about my leathery hands. But that's okay with me because this is our way of life. I like working hard beside my Papa and Mama, helping them and sharing the load of work.

"When will Papa be home? *¿Cuándo regresa mi Papa a mi casa?*" I ask for the tenth time today or maybe in the last hour. *"When, when, when? ¿Cuándo, cuándo, cuándo?"*

I continue to ignore Mama's commands to help her. I jump to my feet. A walk around the house may help the uneasy feeling in my heart.

Slowly I drag my feet as I kick a pebble here and trip over a cow manure chip there--our new house. What an adventure! I love it here and always have, and I love everything about it. The desert plants I like the best are the sagebrush and the *cholla* cactus. I love the smell of the sagebrush and the hot pink flowers on the *cholla*. We often see antelope, buffalo, jackrabbits, deer, and roadrunners.

Spring is my favorite season with the high desert plants blooming. The colors are amazing—red, green, yellow and pink. The gramma and buffalo grass green up, the *cholla* blooms bright red and pink, and the cows calve. It's in the spring that the wind blows and blows. Dust devils dance across the open plains like children chasing each other.

I catch a whiff of *piñon* or cedar in the spring breeze and relish those smells. Springtime on the high desert is a grand mixture of sights and smells. There are wonderful springtime sounds that I love: meadowlarks twills, a calf bawling for its mama. My favorite is the coyotes howling. When a pack of coyotes howl in the early evening up on the mesa behind our house, the sound sends a chill up and down my spine. I know that they are the enemy for our defenseless calves but the coyote's song captures my wild heart.

Papa has taught me how to live in harmony with the wildlife on the plains, enjoying their presence and only killing them for food, sustenance for our life. There are people around these parts who kill animals for no clear reason. We see many carcasses around. Maybe they think it is fun. They leave them to die. That seems so useless to me.

One time Papa and I were riding up on the mesa behind the house and found a doe shot and left to die. Snuggling close beside the dead mother was a young barely-alive fawn, smelling the unfamiliar odor of death that surrounded this beautiful animal, its only source for life.

I remember Papa's words, *"¡Que lastima!* What a pity! What a waste! That poor fawn will die now because of some fool. Two animals dead because someone was so stupid." Seeing that sad baby next to its dying mother has always brought a lump to my throat. I will never forget it.

I remember many times of not enough food, but Papa never killed any animal unless it was for food or our protection, and we survived.

I squeeze the marble in my clenched fist as I circle the house, wanting to scream. Last month I went with Papa to Trinidad and we stayed with his brother, Miguel. In Trinidad, I had kids to play marbles with, but now--NO ONE! Out here, we do have neighbors that have children but only boys. They don't live really close and the families out here work so hard to keep everything going that there's not much time for children to play. And none of our neighbors' children have marbles or know how to play with them.

That trip spoiled me because I had never been to Trinidad before. I begged Papa to let me go with him this time, but he was insistent that I needed to stay home with Mama. I wonder why?

The sun lowers behind the purple mesa, casting shadows across our land. My circling the house ends when Mama announces that supper is ready. Lost in thought, time had slipped away. Mama lights our kerosene lamp that is the sole source of light in our meager home. The yellow light from the lamp usually warms and delights me. Not tonight.

After cooking dinner, she serves our meal in mutual silence. She is tired of nagging me to help and I am preoccupied with Papa's absence. She is too; she always nags more when Papa isn't here. We both miss him, and we both handle it in our own different ways.

After a long uneventful evening—no time sitting near the arroyo watching wildlife with someone, no songs or games like when Papa is here. After cleaning up after dinner, Mama sits in her chair at the table, mending socks. I stand at the window staring at the familiar sight, lost in thought for most of the evening. I say *"Buenas noches"*—good night to Mama. She repeated that familiar phrase and added her favorite one, *"Tenga buenos sueños, mi hija," and* she closes the door to their bedroom. I put on my nightgown and I go to bed and turn my face to the adobe wall, concentrating on the patterns the straw makes in the adobe plaster.

"I forgot to blow out the lamp," Mama returns to the kitchen and sits at the kitchen table near my bed. The kerosene lamp reflects playful images on the wall that usually intrigue me, but tonight it feels so hollow. She lingers at the table like she wants to talk. Maybe she doesn't want to go to bed alone. I wait; she says nothing. I snuggle in under my quilts piled high upon my bed, hoping that tomorrow will be the day Papa returns. Mama blows out the lamp, comes by my bed and touches my forehead with a quiet *"Te quiero.* I love you." She goes to my parents' bedroom and shuts the door.

The third day finally ends.

nother day starts and continues as the previous three days, and my thoughts occupy my day.

Since moving to the United States from Nuevo Laredo, Mexico in *"el estado,"* the northern state of Monterrey in 1920 and then to Mora, New Mexico in 1921, we have always lived out in the country away from people. It feels safer because we don't speak English; we speak Spanish. Many of the other people we meet don't speak Spanish. We have found Mexicans wherever we have lived, which is reassuring. But Papa likes living out where we are by ourselves. We love the country, the wildlife and the quiet. Usually we have friends within miles of us.

Here in the Branson area, at night you can see the lights of campfires and kerosene lamps dotting the plains, identifying the many homesteads and our neighbors. Many of these neighbors are Mexican too, which is comforting. We help each other out and we do get together once in a while for *un baile,* a dance, or a social event.

We moved here in 1923, and I was three years old. In 1927 Laurence Horner and his family moved to Branson. He started buying up a lot of the land around us because many of the homesteaders decided they couldn't make it out on the plains of southeastern Colorado and northeastern New Mexico. Many of them moved to Trinidad and they kept in contact with Papa and Mama.

Mr. Horner introduced himself to us when he first arrived. We see him on a regular basis because he delivers our mail. He seems friendly enough and tries to visit with us when we do have mail, but he doesn't speak Spanish, so Papa is the only one who can partially communicate with him. It is awkward, but he keeps trying. I hide behind Mama's full skirt during his visits but try to make out these foreign sounds.

Mama hollers at me, wondering where I am. Her shout brings me back to today. I see Paco sunning himself on the front step and scoop him up in my skirt. I duck behind the house and sit with my back against the warm wall. The marble continues rolling around in my hand, and Paco jumps off my leg and wanders away.

Mama is so busy with her work. She would never play marbles with me, anyway. In fact, she probably doesn't know how to play with this little treasure. When I brought it home, she had never seen one. Oh well. I can feel a conflict in my heart begin to grow now. I'm lonesome. I need a playmate, friends, and people, mostly Papa. Yet I love living out here where I can sneak up on a mountain lion perched on a sandstone rock ridge, relishing seeing this beautiful creature out free and wild.

The experience in Trinidad with Papa's family reminded me of our small village, Mora, New Mexico and my friends there. I was three years old when we left, but I do remember regular playmates. I yearn for a friend, someone to play with and to talk to, especially a girl.

In Mora, I did have a girl playmate, Susanna, and we played with our dolls. We dressed up in Mama's shoes and pranced around the house like grown-up women. Mama and Susanna's mother laughed at us, enjoying our mimicking them.

Mama couldn't braid my hair, but Susanna's mother could. I miss that too. My long black hair gets tangled in the wind here on the plains. Mama has tried to learn how to braid, but her fingers just don't work that way.

Rosa, the wife of our neighbor here in Colorado, braids my hair sometimes. She has three sons and loves to pretend that I am her daughter, so she does things like that for me whenever we get together. But not too often, because she is so busy with her family and home.

The knowledge of a world larger than this solitary way that I've known most of my life was rekindled in me last month. When Papa is here, I don't mind it so much, but today it's unbearable. I wonder why it is so different today.

Marbles! That had been my new discovery in Trinidad last month and was I good at playing this new game. This blue one is my favorite. Papa taught me how to play one afternoon in his brother Miguel's back yard. He showed me how to position myself to shoot the best. He curled up his index finger against my thumb and flicked the marble with precision. After a couple times, I had it down. Then I practiced and practiced and beat everyone in my uncle's neighborhood, el *barrio de mi tio.*

Wow, were my boy cousins, *mis primos,* jealous--a girl beating them in marbles! This puzzles me even more, though. I am not like my other girl cousins, *mis primas*: dainty, sissy and giggly. Some say I'm a tomboy, whatever that means. Mama says, "*la niña poco femenina.*" I guess girls are supposed to act one way and boys another. That is strange to me, but I have noticed a difference. I see that when Mama wants me to do housework all the time and not tag along after Papa so much. But I would rather be outside, around the animals and I do well at games like marbles.

Oh well, another mystery of this world that I don't understand. So much is a mystery to me these days. Why do coyotes kill our cute baby calves when there are all kinds of other wild animals around for them to eat? Or why did Mama's baby die last year?

When her belly started growing, I was so shocked when Papa told me that Mama was going to have a baby. A brother or a sister? I squealed with delight--a playmate, finally! I didn't care if it was a boy or girl, just a playmate!

The baby was a big healthy boy; Momma screamed and cried when he came out and we were all so excited. Our neighbor's wife, Rosa, helped Mama deliver the baby. Papa waited outside with me, pacing, talking to himself and wringing his hands.

"*¡Es un hijo! Se llama Tito.*" Papa announced. He shouted with joy when Rosa announced it was a baby boy and finally named him Tito, after my Papa's father in Mexico, *mi abuelo*. His son was finally here! He had waited for years for this moment. I know he cherishes me, but a boy insured that his name would continue now. He would have someone to carry on for him on our place.

Then for no clear reason, my new baby brother stopped breathing, turned blue and died. I wonder why?

Dr. Blackerby, the doctor who lives in Branson, came by to see Mama after this hard loss. He wanted to see that she was physically OK. Some of our neighbors asked him to drop by. Her physical body rebounded but her spirit grieved for years. There finally came a time where she could mention her loss and not sob uncontrollably.

Questions plague me these days. My mind over-flows with them. Life isn't as simple as it used to be when I was younger, before visiting Trinidad. I need to talk to Papa about them. I love sharing my questions and ideas with him because he always listens, never making me feel stupid, but he's gone. And I can't talk to Mama about things like this anymore. She changed after losing her baby.

I don't know if all these questions came from going to Trinidad and seeing a larger world or not. All I know is that my world is changing NOW. I don't feel as comfortable here in this solitary place as I did before. Why?

After another successful day of avoiding Mama's demands to help her in the house, I chalk off another day. I continue the evening routine of the previous three days and go to bed early. A quiet "*Buenas noches*" and a hug from Mama sends me to bed again. I huddle down in the quilts and turn my face to the wall again—that familiar wall! I whisper my nightly litany, "Papa, come home! *¡Papa, ven a casa!*" I slip off to sleep. Maybe tomorrow would bring Papa home and life would return to normal finally.

Finally, the fourth day ends.

## 5
---

Daylight and cheerful meadowlarks wake me early this warm summer morning. I peek into Mama's bedroom, and her quiet rhythmic breathing tells me that she is still asleep. In the silence of the morning, I dress and shut the door behind me. Paco is waiting on the step for me to scoop him up in my skirt and go to the arroyo.

Papa has taught me how to move when we want to see wildlife. He says to walk slow and careful and to stay alert to all around.

Remembering his words, I walk to the edge of the arroyo, wanting to be able to see what is there. Without a sound, I ease myself over the edge of the sandstone arroyo and settle in, Paco and me.

The sandstone rock in the arroyo is cut like

someone layered it. I always enjoy looking at the swirling patterns in the rock. The orange, beige and brown colors mix together and make beautiful patterns. Often I bring a rock home to Mama and she arranges them in our yard in different designs.

I love the crisp cool breeze of the early morning on the prairie. I watch a serene doe water in the reservoir across the arroyo and soothe her spirit. A jackrabbit hops around a *cholla* and stops. His ears perk up, listening for any enemies, and he waits. A buck joins the doe for refreshment and companionship. Time escapes me sitting here. It is a respite from the thoughts that have badgered me the last few days.

After this special quiet time alone with my wild friends and Paco, the troublesome thoughts and questions of yesterday return. Again they tumble around in my head.

The smell of a *piñon* fire lures me back to the house for breakfast. I know Mama is up and breakfast will be ready. She questions me about what animals I saw. I tell her just a doe, a buck, jackrabbit and, of course, Paco. Other mornings my list is longer. She enjoys my morning ritual and participates by asking me what I saw. She never cuts me off in listing what I saw. She likes it all, but she prefers to sleep in instead of getting up early.

After a simple breakfast of beans, tortillas and coffee, I leave Mama to her housework and walk around the house to the corral we built. Smokey, one of our horses, stands there. I love her buckskin coloring—a cream colored coat with dark brown mane and tail and dark brown markings on her feet. I watch as her brown tail switches the bothersome flies, and she stamps her feet as the heel-flies nip at her. Summer is coming and this is going to be a scorching, hot day.

"*Hola,* Smokey." I greet her with a smile as I near her, offering a friendly hand on her nose, so velvety and warm. She whinnies her greeting to me like she does every morning. It's her way to communicate with me, our daily ritual. Smokey neighs anytime I am near. She bumps my hand with her nose, looking for a treat like carrots, but I don't have any. I usually do, but we ran out. I hope Papa remembers to bring some from Trinidad. I had to remind him on the last trip.

The strong pungent smell of horse overcomes me. As I get closer to Smokey, I climb up on the fence and urge her to come to me so I can give her a bear hug around her neck. I love to twirl her dark brown forelock hair between my fingers. She always flicks her head back in a playful manner, telling me to stop.

The smell--so strong as she gets closer and so hard to put into words! Smokey's like a friend to me, my best friend. It seems like she understands me when I tell her my secrets, but her silence bothers me. Sometimes I wish she could talk and tell me what she thinks. Now I just have to guess. Before I talked to my playmates in Trinidad, this didn't bother me, but it does now. My cousins, *mis primos,* talked and talked and talked. It was so much fun. We didn't talk about anything important, but we talked. I struggle with this quandary: I love our solitary life on the high plains of Colorado, but I miss playmates.

When Papa and I ride together, Smokey's my mount, always. She's a good cow horse, doesn't spook at much and is well trained. Papa trained her, himself. Smokey is especially good as a cutting horse, like Papa's horse. When we bring the cattle in to work them, we may need to separate a sick cow out of the herd. Smokey goes after the cow I identify and does all the work. I grip the reins and the saddle horn and just go along for the ride.

Papa's horse is a sorrel—a copper reddish coat

with a white marking on his face. He named him "Rusty" because of his coloring. His horse is the best cutting horse of the two. Both of our horses have a natural instinct for cutting.

We got Smokey when she was a colt two years ago and I raised her myself—you could say she is my filly. I enjoyed helping Papa halter break her. I would spend long hours leading her around the corral, singing in her ear. At first she would be stubborn and not want to follow me, so Papa would have to help me pull her along. She wanted to go back to her Momma, but eventually she got over that. She would balk, then run out to end of the line. Finally she realized what I wanted her to do, so she joined me without a fight.

One of the best parts about riding with Papa is that he lets me wear jeans and boots; otherwise, I wear a dress made out of an old flour sack. The jeans protect my legs from the rough leather on the saddle. The jeans and boots also protect me from the shrub oak and the rattlesnakes that are plentiful on the high plains of Colorado. Last summer, Papa killed twenty rattlesnakes. That was twice as many as the year before. We have never had anyone of us bit by a snake; Papa is proud of that fact. We see them often, but no bites.

My times riding with Papa are my favorites. We never know what's going to happen when we ride. One day we were rounding up some cows and calves down by a huge cottonwood tree by the reservoir. For no clear reason, Smokey spooked at something I guess in the tree and started to run away. She caught me off guard, so my hands jerked out to the ends of the reins and I lost control of her head. She loped at full speed around the tree three or four times with me holding on for dear life.

Papa kept hollering to me, "Get down on your reins. Her head is completely free." I was sure that I would end up on the ground, but I didn't. Whatever started Smokey on this wild adventure ended as quickly as it started. When she stopped, I tightened my grip on her reins and was in control again.

In a cloud of dust Papa rode up to me laughing and concerned, "Well, *mi hijita*, you did pretty good. You didn't hit the ground." I always remember that as a compliment. I felt like Papa accepted me as a pretty good rider that day, and that was important to me. I always tried to please him. He was a man of few words, so this comment meant a lot. I could tell him anything and he would not yell at me or lecture me.

Lost in my remembering with Smokey, I am startled when I hear horse hooves behind me. As I turn around, I squeal with delight. Through a swirling dust cloud, Papa sits on his horse high above me, smiling. Papa is finally home after the longest four days of my life!

Everything is right again.

## 6

"*Ven aqui, mi hijita!*" He bellows his favorite endearment to come to him. I rush towards him before he can jump off his horse.

"How's Trinidad, Papa? *¿Cómo están mis primos?* How are my cousins? How is *mi tio* Miguel, my uncle?" I shoot questions at him as he jumps down from his horse and draws me into a tight bear hug.

"I missed you so. Mama won't go riding with me. I saw some coyotes yesterday heading for the calves and I'm sure we need to check out the herd. Don't leave me again. Do you hear me? It's so lonesome here without you. I missed you so! But I thought you were going to be gone for a week. Why are you back so soon?" The words tumble out of my mouth as one long, unpunctuated sentence.

"Well, well, Shorty, sounds like you need your old man around here," Papa says with a proud twinkle in his eyes. Something strange happens then. An unfamiliar shadow crosses those sparkling eyes. "Let's unsaddle this horse and go talk with Mama. Uh, I finished quicker than usual in Trinidad--that's why I'm home early."

I grab the reins and walk beside Papa holding his big, rough hand in my small hand. My world is safe and secure again. As a team, we unsaddle the horse, enjoying a special communion of quietness. Papa hangs the saddle and bridle up on the wooden fence post. He casually throws his saddlebag up on the fence. The horse is sweaty and thirsty from the long hard ride. I want to brush him down, but I struggle because of my size.

Papa fills a bucket with water from the arroyo and brings it back to water his horse. Out of the corner of my eye, I see that he watches me work. He has taught me everything I know about caring for our horses. Papa grabs me a stool so I can brush and curry comb his horse. Remember my nickname is Shorty and I am eight years old. He supervises my care with pride. He turns away from me to wipe his eyes and grabs the saddle, the blanket and bridle. "Maria, let's put this in the saddle room. Give me the brush and the curry comb and let's go."

I push open the door to the saddle room and Papa places the saddle blanket on the saddle rack. With caution, we look around the saddle room for rattlesnakes. They love to curl up inside of a saddle, so we always check the whole area out. With ease, he tosses the saddle up on the rack and hangs the bridle on a hook above the saddle. My saddle and gear are next to his.

"I'll beat you to the house," Papa says over his shoulder as he sprints out the door of the saddle room. He ducks around the corner and waits so I can catch him.

As I fly by him, he giggles and screams, "I can't ever beat you." I increase my speed and dart in the door of our house, laughing and overflowing with love for this wonderful man.

"He's home--he's home! *El está en casa--el está en casa!*" I sing as I dance in a circle around Mama. The glow in her eyes welcomes Papa home as they embrace and exchange special whispers.

"This little girl has been terrible--missing you like a lost puppy. You spoil her too much!" Mama says with a chuckle that shows a mixture of pride and joy in her voice. Her eyes dart to the side as she

remembers how Papa also spoiled her with the friv-
olous purchase of a fainting couch last year.

Papa drove his horse and wagon to Trinidad after
we sold our cattle on a mission. He had spied this
beautiful fainting couch in the window of the furniture store on Commercial Street. He brought it back
to Mama so proud of his purchase. She affirms in
her heart, "He does spoil '*los mujeres*,' the women, in
his life."

"I'm glad you're home, too. I've missed you." The
words echo what I've already said, but Papa receives
them in a different manner from her. He cuddles her
in his arms and kisses her on the lips, holding her
tight for several minutes. Mama buries her face in
his strong shoulder and relishes his embrace.

The peaceful atmosphere of Papa's homecoming
changes. I notice a tension and a strain in both of
their eyes. This quiet communication excludes me.

Mama whispers, "*¿Qué has descubierto en
Trinidad?* What did you find out in Trinidad?" These
words seem to cut like a knife through Papa's face.

"We'll discuss it later. Well, just a moment, Maria,
go check my saddlebags. I do believe there's a
surprise in one of them for *mi hijita*." I loved it when
he called me "*mi hijita*"--his special little daughter. As
he finishes the sentence, I race out the door and

scramble up the fence to search Papa's saddlebags, finding a sack of marbles. The bag spills out on the dirt: cat eyes, stripes—my hands full of color.

My heart fills with joy. I burst into the house to shower Papa with "thank-you, gracias" kisses and hugs. But my flight into childish ecstasy crashes to the ground. Papa turns his head to hide what I had already seen, tears streaming down his face, fear in his eyes and a soul-twisting anguish on his face I had never seen before.

Mama wipes her own shower of tears away with the edge of her grimy apron and encircles both of us into her trembling arms, repeating midst the sobs and tears, "*Mi hijita, mi esposo*, what will we do? *¡Mi Dios me ayuda, por favor!* My God, please help me!"

Mama's plea for God's help scares me because she only says that when something horrible has happened. I didn't understand. What had destroyed our peaceful, wonderful world while I was retrieving my gift? Finally I wrestle free from Mama's grip and run into Papa's open arms. His body shakes with the deep, violent sobs of a man torn to pieces.

"*¡Dígame, Papa, Dígame!*" I instruct Papa to tell me what's happening and join in the contagious weeping that surrounds me. Papa kneels down in front of me, eye-to-eye. I look into the wonderful, loving eyes of the man who has always cared for me, but this time total despair replaces his customary smile and twinkle.

"*Mi hijita*, some men, *gringos malos*, say that I stole two horses from them and that I must go to jail. But it is not true, it is a lie, *un mentira!* I don't know what to do--they will come after me, I'm sure! I can't leave you and your mother. *No la puedo dejar tu* y *tú madre.* I am not a horse thief. *Yo no soy un ladron de caballos.*"

These words fall from his lips in a deep sob, and I try to understand. "My Papa, a horse thief, *un ladron de caballos*? No way! Will they hang him?" I know the truth. The only horses we have are Smokey and Papa's horse, Rusty. He bought both; I raised Smokey from a colt. I went with him to pick the colt out of the herd at Rose's Horse Ranch. None of this makes sense. I can't comprehend it, and I can't understand his not just telling them so!

But reality hits. Papa can only speak broken English, not enough to explain his innocence. Mama and I can speak only Spanish, so language stops us all from communicating outside of our people.

And these people--these accusers--care nothing about our language problems. *¡Mi Papa es no un ladron de caballos!* My Papa is not a horse thief!

## 7

---

Our language issue has been a problem since we moved to the United States. I first remember hearing English when we lived in Mora, New Mexico and had gone to Las Vegas, New Mexico for groceries and supplies. I was shocked. Papa told me that it was *ingles*, the language of the United States. It sounded so different, yet I recognized a few words—they sounded similar to words in my own language. How could that be?

Why then would we move here to the United States, facing isolation because of this language barrier?

The Mexican Revolution broke out in 1910 when Francisco I. Madero, a reformist writer and politician challenged the dictatorship of President Porfirio Díaz which had gone on for decades. Madero wanted clean elections, but Diaz refused. He liked controlling the elections and the people. Three leaders answered Madero's call for the revolution: Emiliano Zapata lived in the south, and Pascual Orozco and Pancho Villa lived in the north. Because my parents lived in the northern part of Mexico, they knew more about Orozco and Villa; about Zapata, they just heard rumors.

Villa and Orozco rose in power under Madero. Díaz was deposed in 1911, but the revolution was just beginning. By the time it ended, millions had died, caught in the middle as rival politicians and warlords fought each other over the cities and regions of Mexico.

By 1920, a farmer and revolutionary general Alvaro Obregón rose to the presidency by outliving his main rivals. I heard Papa and his friends say that this event marked the end of the revolution, although the violence continued well into the 1920's.

My parents felt they had to move because the Mexican Revolution had torn up our country and we had lost many members of our family and friends. Papa hated the violence and feared for his life. Men joined Pancho Villa to stop President Porfirio Diaz's rule. They joined Villa each time the leadership changed, but it was so confusing to know whom to believe.

Papa was fortunate that he survived the battles he was in. He came home one night after Pancho Villa started another campaign, saying, "We must go to El Norte—go north to America—for freedom and safety." The three leaders—Zapata, Orozco, and Villa—were fighting amongst themselves. Papa knew we needed to get out of Mexico, and his best friend Pablo agreed with him.

So Pablo, Rosa and their family joined us. Papa's brother, Miguel who lived in Trinidad, had escaped with his family years earlier and had been writing encouraging letters to Papa to get out and come to America. Literate friends read these hopeful notes to Papa and Mama.

They left northern Mexico early in the spring in 1920 with Mama pregnant with me. This wasn't the best timing because she was eight months along and miserable. The trip across the border was difficult. The desire to move north into the United States grew in Papa as I grew inside of Mama.

They crossed the border into Laredo, Texas from Nuevo Laredo, Mexico and stayed in the southern Texas area until I was born March 20, 1920. They stayed there for a month so Mama could heal. Mama said that I traveled easily. I am sure they wondered how a month-old baby would behave, but numerous times they recounted to me that the rocking of the wagon lulled me to sleep most of the way.

Then they decided to move farther north to be farther from the border. They kept hearing rumors of Pancho Villa and his raids and it scared Papa. Papa and Mama worked their way north through Texas. There were many nights of sleeping under the stars, migrating farther and farther north, eventually into New Mexico.

Papa knew that the hand of the Mexican Revolution had extended into southern New Mexico at Columbus during January 1916 with Villa kidnapping and killing 18 people. He wanted away from that way of life—he wanted free of the fear and the violence, so he moved to northern New Mexico.

In 1921, Papa and Mama ended up at Mora, New Mexico, a quaint Mexican village in northeastern New Mexico, situated in a lush green valley, surrounded by the Sangre de Cristo mountains. The Mora River wove its way through the valley nourishing wildlife and farms along its bank. Pablo and Rosa moved with us. Many Mexicans who had settled there welcomed us.

Mora resides in a beautiful, fertile valley where

farming and ranching flourish. Papa worked hard there, learning how to operate a ranch and how to farm. This was foreign to him, but he took to it immediately. He prided himself in saving a calf and its mother in a hard birth or stacking the hay in neat rows at the end of the season.

As wonderful as this place was, there was a deep lure to go farther north for Papa. He remembered that Pancho Villa had stepped foot into this state, and he wanted farther away. When friends would gather, stories of Felipe Baca going north in 1862 with twelve families were told and retold. Papa became enamored with the idea of moving to Colorado where he could have his own place. He discussed it with Pablo and they decided it was time to move north. Papa and Mama packed up everything we owned and loaded the wagon for the trip north.

It was hard for Papa and Mama to leave their newfound friends, but Papa wanted to get as far north as possible, so away we went. What eased the pain of leaving was his best friend, Pablo, and his family joined us. Also his brother lived in Trinidad, and he was anxious to see him again—it had been years.

Felipe had ended up being the founder of

Trinidad, but Pablo and Papa both wanted to start a ranch. We followed the old Santa Fe Trail north but instead of going over Raton Pass, we took a southern route through Emery Gap and ended up in Branson, CO.

Branson had been a thriving small community at the railhead of the railroad, but two fires in 1921 and 1922 had wiped out many businesses. When we arrived, it was small and offered few businesses for our needs.

Papa and Pablo headed their families east of Branson on a dusty dirt road and found our land and homesteaded it.

It's an amazing story how we got here, to the place we love and now these wild accusations!

Papa sighs and stops his tears. He goes out the door as normal as possible to feed the livestock, saying to Mama over his shoulder "*Tengo hambre.* I'm hungry. What's for supper?"

Joining his efforts to establish some normalcy, Mama tries to compose herself and giggles at his statement of hunger and his question about supper. Our mundane menu remains pretty much the same every night: homemade tortillas, frijoles, antelope or venison that Papa has shot. His question always tickles Mama and today prompts a smile from her as always, even in the midst of this chaos. Tonight, she sighs at his effort to return to our normal routine but fears that it will never be the same again.

As I step out the front door and head around the house to help Papa, the setting sun blinds me. I stop to enjoy the beauty of the day's end, my favorite time. Today, we are later than normal. Usually by now, Papa and I have finished with the chores, enjoying this time together, sitting in silence on the ridge near the watering hole to see what wildlife will come in to water. Will it be a visit from a deer, a skunk, a bear or a porcupine? Papa always says to stop and experience what surrounds us, that we are lucky to live in such a beautiful place.

Drawn by my habit and the beauty of the cool of the day, I stop and watch the sunset. Tonight colorful clouds fill the western sky and the sun has painted them purple, blue and orange—an explosion of color on the horizon. The disappearing sun outlines the mesa, turning it a darker and darker shade of purple. Far away a coyote yelps at a mate or offspring. The wind that always blows on the plains stirs up a dust devil and I race to escape the shower of dirt.

Everything seems the same, like so many other days spent on these barren plains. Maybe, just maybe, Papa is wrong, scared for nothing. Maybe the men were just teasing him. The *gringos* love to tease us Mexicans; it's like a game with them. There's a tension existing between them and my people. I don't understand why, but they scare me. I can't understand them and those that bother us don't speak Spanish.

From our Mexican friends who spoke more English, I have heard stories of horse thieves in the area, but I never paid much attention to them. The historical term used often for a horse thief is a "Dutch Henry," a term I did know in English. I had heard that mobs running the area hung most horse thieves. Law and order was not a strong power in this area; mobs were. I always thought of them as bad men and didn't want to have anything to do with them or their stories.

Papa's yelling interrupts my thoughts, "¡*Mi hijita, ayúdame*! Come help me! I need your help."

Brought back to reality by his voice, I bolt toward the corral. I shake off the thoughts crowding my mind, knowing that my world is ok and back to normal. Papa is home, and he needs my help.

# 8
---

Papa and I finish our daily chores and head for the house, hungry and ready to eat. Papa spots a five-point buck and three does. Their movement is slow and graceful. They are in no hurry to travel to the water hole east of our house. He signals me to be quiet and grabs my hand. We ease down the ridge to watch these free, beautiful animals water and graze in the cool of the evening. Their silhouettes stand out as the last rays of sunshine etch their forms against the ground.

Papa squats down on a sandstone rock ledge that overlooks the watering hole, and his rough hands encircle me as I squat in front of him. I can feel his heavy breathing on the back of my neck and smell the familiar aroma of his sweaty clothes mixed with horse and leather. I so enjoy these special times together.

He surprises me with a tight squeeze, stands up and walks towards the house in front of me. He drags his feet and the dust stirs up in small clouds. I see the nape of his neck, tanned by long hours in the sun. Tonight it is tense and tight with the load of his world.

We sit down to supper with an unusual silence hanging over our table. We try small talk about Papa's trip to Trinidad and what happened here in his absence. Each of us jumps at any strange sound outside during the meal, fearing the unknown. Mama lights the kerosene lantern, placing it in the middle of the table to illumine our dark kitchen. The anxious mood lingers in the dim amber light.

Usually the yellow light from the kerosene lamp comforts me in our long evenings inside our house. The shadows dancing on the walls have become good friends and playmates, but tonight it is so different. The dark, forbidding forms on the walls add to the suspense, feeling evil and scary.

Halfway through our delicious, but modest meal, the much-feared event happens. Horses approach our house in a rush of noise from men and animals. The dreaded moment arrives and catches us all clustered together in the dark corner of our small kitchen. Three unfinished meals cover our deserted table.

Several loud men on nondescript sweaty, panting horses ride up with shouting and cussing. A brisk pounding at the door sends us further in the corner. Before Papa can open the door, this mob forces the door open. What a violent invasion of our home! Six *gringos* fill our small, modest house of stone and adobe with their foreign language and foreign smells. One of these invaders is the sheriff of Las Animas County.

Peering from behind Mama's protective full skirt, I see the sheriff-- now our enemy--argue with Papa in English. Papa pleads. I don't understand the words, but I do understand the tone of his voice and theirs. Grabbing the sheriff's hand, he begs, pleads, and cries! And then, they laugh, a communication that crosses all languages. Their laughter overflows with power, ridicule and anger. And all this is aimed at my Papa, my hero! That laughter bounces off of our adobe walls and crashes into my head.

The sheriff and one man get on each side of Papa and push him outside towards the corrals. The others move back to their horses, light cigarettes and stand talking. Mama and I move closer to the closed door, listening and trying to understand what is happening. I don't understand their words but I know they feel they have won.

In a loud voice, Papa continues to argue with the two men who take him to the corral where the horses are. I hear English words that I do know: "The Rose horse ranch" where we bought Smokey as a colt. From the conversation, I see in my mind the two *gringos* surveying our two horses, especially Papa's horse. Papa continues his litany of innocence with his voice growing louder and shriller with each statement, but they ignore him. Laughter is their only response.

I hear Papa beg about something. The two ruffians bring him back to the house for our tearful good-bye. The last thing I remember hearing is his screams as they drag him from our house. *"¡Mi hijita, mi esposa preciosa--espérame, espérame!"* His screams for us to wait for him echo through my mind. I must have fainted because the next thing I remember is waking to Mama and our neighbor and friend, Pablo, standing over me with worried looks on their faces.

"Where's Papa? Where's Papa? *¿Dónde está mi Papa?*" I scream, demanding to know and trying to shake the cobwebs of uncertainty from my mind.

Mama falls across me on my small bed, crying and sobbing out of control, "¡*Papa, se ha ido!* Papa's gone! He's gone. *Se lo llevaron.* They took him away." The weight of her body and sound of her wails almost suffocate me.

Pushing Mama aside, I scramble out from underneath her, search our two-room home and explode. Uncontrollable anger rages from deep within me and I attack and destroy anything I can get my hands on. My doll crashes against the hard rock wall; my marbles fly out the door in all directions.

Mama tries to console me in the midst of my savage tantrum, but I push her away. I shove open the front door and collapse on the front step. I scream, I cry, and I wail! Finally, I take a breath and open my eyes—Paco is staring at me a few feet away. He seems apprehensive about coming any closer. My tantrum has lost its power, so my little friend ventures near and I scoop him up in my skirt. I gingerly hold him in my hand while my sobs are subsiding. He seems to know that I need him close to me. I sit there with him consoling me.

I look around and see my marbles strewn around our front door; I don't pick them up, but go inside, leaving Paco outside. Mama and Pablo stop their conversation, and I slide into my bed fully dressed.

Pablo touches my brow with gentle rough fingers and whispers, "*Adios. Hasta la mañana.*" I appreciate his good-bye and the hope of seeing him tomorrow. Mama walks to the door with him and says her good-byes.

She returns to my bed and repeats what Pablo did; she touches my brow with her long slender fingers and whispers, "*Buenas noches.*" Tonight her good night doesn't bless my heart like usual. With a sob, she adds, "*Tenga buenos sueños,*" but I'm sure I will not have good dreams tonight. I sigh my response and turn to the wall, heart-broken because the most valuable person in my life has been taken away.

I toss and turn the whole night. Mama must have sensed my restless because she came and slept with me, snuggled in close and tight in my twin bed.

Our world had been shattered that night, so we held on to each other, trying to make sense of the insanity.

---

## 9

That horrible scene happened in 1928 and haunted me for years. It would wake me up drenched in sweat, screaming and feeling like the weight of Mama's body across me. I felt like her shrill wailing would suffocate me.

What happened after this horrible monumental night? The sheriff and those ruthless men threw Papa into jail in Trinidad, and he faced a ten-year sentence for horse stealing. Because of the language barrier, he received no defense. His sentence was an unusually long sentence for the crime. Most convicted horse thieves received a one- to five-year sentence. Many years later, I realized he was a victim of prejudice and mob rule in the Trinidad area.

"Dutch Henry" became a phrase I hated because

his accusers used it often to describe my precious Papa.

Mama and I were not at his trial; we had no way to get there. Neither of us felt that we could add anything to his defense, and he did not want us there. He was so ashamed and broken. But we desperately wanted to be there and spent many nights at our kitchen table in the glow of that yellow kerosene lamp, crying and trying to understand Papa's refusal to see us.

I didn't understand it. I ached to see him and touch him and smell him, but he continually refused to see us before and after his trial. Miguel, his brother, and family in Trinidad tried to help, but they had limited funds and also had to deal with the language issue, too. They had been in the United States longer, but they still did not have a command of the English language. The atmosphere surrounding Papa's imprisonment in Trinidad was volatile so the sheriff moved Papa to a larger jail in northern Colorado in a place named Greeley after Papa was sentenced.

Many of our Mexican friends wanted to do something to get Papa out of jail, but again language barriers stopped them. Rumors bounced around Trinidad and the small communities in the area about a plan to bust Papa out of jail. Rumors are all they were. Our hands were tied. No our tongues were tied!

For a couple years Mama and I tried to keep the homestead going. Pablo and many other good friends tried to help. We did pretty well for a while, but eventually it became too much. Without my horse, I couldn't do the work needed to take care of our cattle or the homestead.

A week after taking Papa, the sheriff returned and gave Mama an official paper explaining Papa's crime and his sentence. It was in English of course. We asked one of our friends to translate it for us. Mama kept that paper in her special place under the bed because it identified Papa's release date—June 27, 1938.

Our neighbors, Pablo and Rosa, shared their food with us. We shared the workload of both homesteads. Papa had trained me well to be a good hand, but we so needed horses. A month after the sheriff's last visit, he came and took our two horses. What were we to do?

Pablo only had three horses, enough for him and his two oldest boys, so I traded off with the younger of the two older boys to do the work I could do. Pablo's youngest son couldn't help on the place yet because he was too small—and not enough horses.

We sold our calves that fall. It was 1928 and we were able to buy food supplies for the winter, but it was a hard winter. The workload of two places for Pablo was too much. We knew it.

Mama's despair grew and grew in the darkness and cold of that winter. She knew we could not continue in this manner. She included me in the decision-making process. We tried to find work in Branson for Mama, but there was none.

I was beyond school age and finally started school in Branson with all my Mexican friends. Pablo's oldest son was my age, so Pablo drove us to town every day in his wagon.

This was a time of change in transportation in southeastern Colorado. Many of the ranchers had cars; we still used horses and wagons to get around. We couldn't afford a car and it wouldn't work readily in the ruts of our dirt roads.

I hadn't started to school at six like all the other children because Papa needed me to help on the homestead. Now Mama and I realized I needed to learn English to survive in this American world.

I loved the small country school in Branson, and a certain teacher realized the problem the Mexican students had. I was lucky to get her for my first year of school. When this teacher found out that I was eight years old and just starting school, she gave me extra help during lunch and recess. I so appreciated her compassion. Her kindness led me to trust her, which was hard for me to do after Papa's experience. I had trouble trusting any *gringos*.

It was not all wonderful in Branson. Many of the gringo students teased me about my "Dutch Henry" father. Those words cut through me like a knife. Would I ever be able to escape? Would I ever be able to look people in the eye without shame about my Papa?

After a couple years struggling on the homestead, it finally became too much for Mama. We wanted to move to Branson because of its size and our friends that lived close by, but there were no jobs there for Mama, so we had to move to Trinidad.

In 1930, we sold our homestead and acreage to Mr. Horner who had the land adjacent to ours. We had become friends with him because we saw him so often when he delivered our mail. He tried to help us out. He was the first gringo to lend us a hand at all. Mama and I still couldn't understand his English, but we did understand his kind gestures. He brought us eggs each Monday. After his acts of generosity, several people in the Branson community reached out to us in a variety of ways with extra food, rides to Trinidad when we needed them and general aid. It was so nice of the community, but it went against our work ethics; we had to take care of ourselves.

Mama realized that she had to provide for us now that Papa was in jail. I was ten when we moved, frightened to death because I had never lived in a city the size of Trinidad. All I knew was the wide-open plains and the small town of Branson. Mama got a job as a housekeeper for Mr. Riley, a wealthy rancher that lived in Trinidad. Miguel, Papa's brother, helped Mama get the job that saved our lives. I helped out in the house as much as I could, but I never liked it. My heart remained on the open, dry prairie, beside Papa.

What an experience for a young girl! I lost my Papa. He went to jail. I didn't see him again until he was released from prison--ten years later. I was eight when I last saw him and eighteen when he was released.

TEN YEARS OF WAITING! That part of my life remains a blur to me today. I existed. We lived in a small adobe casita behind Mr. Riley's house near Simpson's Rest, a prominent landmark near Trinidad. This mesa ridge jutted out from the rest of the mountain range and comforted my heart because I missed our mesas edging the prairie near our homestead.

Our two-room home was small but comfortable.

At first, Mama and I shared a bed, but eventually we bought a twin bed for me and put it in the corner of our kitchen, just like in our adobe and rock home. We brought most of our stuff from the homestead, so it felt familiar. It was about the same size as our beautiful homestead house, but the view wasn't the same. Our view was the back of Mr. Riley's house, no mesas, no deer, and no openness.

When we first moved to Trinidad, I felt caged and suffered from panic attacks. I would lose my breath and feel like I was suffocating. Mama held and comforted me each time it hit. After awhile, the episodes stopped. I wondered about those episodes for years.

Mr. Riley was so good to Mama and me. Often, he joked with me. He had the best sense of humor. After watching me, he would say, "I know you are hurting. I know you miss your Papa. Get educated and help your parents. Help your people." He knew what had happened to Papa and saw it for what it was: unfair treatment! He had many Mexican friends, and the Mexican community saw him as a fair man and a friend.

I attended private schools, Trinidad Catholic schools, because Mr. Riley had a soft spot in his heart for me and paid for it.

But most of all, I waited. At first, Papa and the prairie was all I thought about. I escaped to the safe, secure past, enjoying and reliving the happy days with Papa riding our horses out on the prairie, taking care of our cattle and enjoying any wildlife that crossed our path.

*Tio*, Uncle Miguel helped ease the pain with regular visits, and he invited Mama and me to spend time with his family. So every Sunday, we went to Mass and afterwards had dinner with *Tio* Miguel's family and played games. His resemblance to Papa helped ease the pain some. I could see Papa's smile in Miguel's eyes and his chuckle was Papa's. I loved that sound.

I did enjoy that part of living in Trinidad. I got to know Papa's family, but that was all that was good about city living. I felt corralled. Sometimes I couldn't breathe. I couldn't hear the coyotes howl or watch the deer graze and water in the evenings. City people were so busy at dusk, which was my favorite time to stop and go to the arroyo and watch for wildlife.

Town people were hard to get to know, and I didn't know where to start. Trinidad did have many Spanish-speaking people, and that comforted me, but the *gringos* scared me. I loved hearing Spanish spoken when Mama and I passed friends on Commercial Street.

But *gringos* gathered on the corner of Main and Commercial streets and mocked us as we walked by. Often I heard the name, "Dutch Henry" hurled at us as we walked by and then an explosion of laughter.

What separated me most from those people in the city was language. At first, I didn't speak or understand English much, and many of them didn't understand Spanish. With one foot in my old secure world and one foot in this new one, I was caught between two worlds.

During this time, one fact kept gnawing at me: my father was innocent. I knew where each of our horses had come from. This knowledge caused a strong emotion to grow in me--a hatred for all *gringos*, whites." I felt that they all were responsible for taking my Papa away from me for no reason. Somehow I had put this all together, either from gossip I had overheard from my family or from other sources, but mostly from the truth that I knew deep inside. This truth was later confirmed, but not soon enough.

After a short time of living in Trinidad and going to school, I became proficient at English because I realized the disadvantage my Papa had by not being able to speak English. The extra help I received in the Branson School from my compassionate teacher started me off on a path of learning that would change my life. If Papa could have spoken and understood English, he might have been able to defend himself, not only to those cruel six men, but also to the judge that laid that exaggerated ten-year sentence on him. My hatred became focused on this unfair man and his rationale, and this hatred accelerated my desire to learn English and become more than proficient at it!

Uncle, *Tio* Miguel explained to Mama and me what the gringo term "Dutch Henry" meant, "That's the slang that the locals use to call a horse thief, and they used it again and again at his trial."

The crazy part is that Dutch Henry had been thieving in the 1880's, so it didn't make any sense. That was years ago! I wonder if Dutch Henry had burned the judge's family before him somehow. I pondered that possibility repeatedly.

Yes, I saw learning English as a vehicle of revenge, of getting back or at least becoming even and equal. These seeds of hatred grew and replaced my love for the prairie that had filled my heart for years. I blocked out the memories of the good times on the plains and in our home and concentrated on survival in my new world in Trinidad with my new language, English. I schemed and planned for my future--I would not end up like my Mama doing menial housework, depending on others to survive or end up like my Papa in jail.

This hatred became the motivating force that kept me going.

But back to the waiting, the endless waiting for ten long years.

## 11

W hat made the years seem endless was not seeing Papa while he was in jail. That never made sense to me, but Papa refused to see Mama or me at all. He was so ashamed about being in jail and he couldn't bear to have us see him behind bars.

Mama and I were stubborn, though. Many times, we would ride with *Tio* Miguel to the jail to see Papa, but he refused to see us. He would see his brother but not us. After the visit, *Tio* Miguel would describe Papa's appearance and attitude as we drove home. Mama and I would whimper the whole way home. There came a time when we stopped going with him. Miguel would report Papa's condition and that would soothe the ache in our hearts until his next visit in a month or so. Even though we stopped going with *Tio* Miguel, I hoped beyond hope that Papa would contact us and ask us to come. It never happened.

As a child, I could not understand why Papa wouldn't see us. I just felt rejected. It did not make sense, but now as an adult I understand. I remember his attitude about life and freedom. Yet the little girl who had spent every day possible of her short life by his side knew only one thing: her father was gone and didn't want to see her. This caused such a mixture of emotions. I missed him so much, yet I hated him, too. I vacillated between sobbing from missing him so much and screaming angry words at him for refusing to see me. What a confused young lady I was!

My relationship with Mama was as convoluted. At first, all Mama did was cry, sitting on her fainting couch in their bedroom at the homestead. She would stroke the couch and repeat, "He bought this for me. He loves me. *Me quiere.* Why, God? *¿Por qué, Dios?* Why? *¿Por qué?*"

She cooked no meals. I sat on my bed in the far corner of the kitchen, dazed by Papa's absence and wounded by Mama's neglect. In those initial days, the only thing that saved us was Pablo and his wife, Rosa. They came over twice a day bringing food in the morning and evening. What happened to our cattle?

I guess Pablo cared for them too. It's all a blur. What happened to the money from the cattle that first year? I am sure that Pablo took care of it for us.

Mama finally came to her senses and started preparing meals, but there was a minimal amount of interaction between us. If we started talking, Papa came up in the conversation and we both started sobbing. I would run down to the arroyo and curl up in a ball in one of the sandstone caves. I screamed, I cried, it felt good, like a release.

The hours grew into days, the days into weeks and months. Our routine was bland, but at least we started one. Mama took care of my basic needs; I helped Pablo take care of our cattle.

One month after the *gringo* mob took Papa, the sheriff and a deputy returned and took our two horses. The scene was heart wrenching. The sound of the horse hooves catapulted Mama and me back to that horrible night and we hid in the corner of our kitchen. Again, they shoved open the door and invaded our home. Again they spewed English words at us. Neither of us had any idea what they were saying.

Pablo just happened to check in on us about the

same time and realized someone was in the corral bothering our two horses. I ventured out the door to see what they were doing and joined Pablo. I would not hide in the corner again. Mama hid in the corner, curled up in a fetal position. She couldn't go through this again, I would not hide again.

When the sheriff bridled Smokey, I screamed and ran towards the corral, but Pablo grabbed my wrist and stopped me. "Maria, stop! *¡Basta!* There's nothing we can do. *No hay nada que podamos hacer.*"

I struggled free, but he captured me from behind. I screamed and hollered, desperate to get to Smokey, my friend, and save him from these horrible men, but Pablo wouldn't let me go. I struggled and struggled but he held onto me. Exhausted from my battle, I crumpled to the ground in a heap, sobbing. As the men rode off with our two horses, laughing and mocking my pain and sorrow, I heard Smokey whinny to me. She knew something was wrong. That whinny echoed through my mind for years.

Mama was absent from that scene. With tears streaming down his face, Pablo picked me up and carried me back inside to her. She was reciting the Rosary in the corner; I sat at the table, crushed by this loss. Pablo stayed an hour or so to console us, but no words could help. Our horses were gone.

How could we manage our homestead without them? My best friend was gone; my Papa was gone. What could I do? How many cattle did Papa have? How would I continue keeping our homestead together? How could I do the work without Smokey?

I faced the adult responsibility of running our homestead. I had to make it work. These questions haunted me for weeks and months.

Before the sheriff took Smokey, my reprieve came when I stepped up into the stirrup and slid into my saddle. We galloped across the open plains with the mesa to my left side, with no destination in mind. I just needed fresh air, the outside and this animal beneath me running. I followed the edge of the mesa, a familiar and comforting boundary for me. I screamed, I cried, it felt good, like a release. Smokey somehow knew I needed our time alone and seemed to cry with me.

## 12

---

"When's Papa coming home? How many years, how many months, how many days left?" became my constant question of poor Mama. At first her response was silence, but after a few years she would answer me, year in and year out. 1938.

I remember when it was seven years and that seemed like forever. "Three years gone. How can I last seven more?" whizzed through my head. Somehow I did, though.

Poor Mama went through the motions of living, but I knew she was counting the days until he came home. She worked so hard to feed and clothe us and never complained.

At first, it was too painful to talk about Papa, so

in our denial, silence filled the room. That first couple of years we avoided the topic, denying anything ever happened. But after a while, we eased into talking about Papa, and sometimes I could enjoy the sharing of our time together, the three of us. Our memories of Papa kept us going.

Late at night I would hear her whimper alone in her bedroom. Somehow I realized this was the hardest time of the day for her, sleeping alone. I can't separate those years; they blend into one long, horrible haze.

Grade school in Trinidad came and went. I started the first grade at eight years old in Branson. By the time we moved to Trinidad, I was ten and in the second grade. My second grade teacher passed me two grades so I could be with my cousins, *mis primos*, that were my age. My teacher felt that *mis primos* would help me advance faster if I were in the same grade with them. My cousins were my only friends in grade school. I kept close to Mama and Miguel's family, still so afraid of the *gringos*.

I did return to playing marbles though. Mr. Riley bought me a bag for my ninth birthday and I practiced in the back yard. He helped me regain my skills before I played my cousins.

The first time I played them, I won. It reminded me of the trip with Papa to Trinidad so long ago, and it made me sad. I gave the marbles to my cousins and hid behind a big cottonwood tree crying, realizing I just couldn't play with them and not remember Papa. It hurt too much.

I continued to learn and grow. After learning to read, I read all the time I could. Many nights Mama would come to my bed and say, "Maria, go to sleep." I was lost in the book and had lost track of time.

Junior high was a chore, but I was a good student, determined to excel and show the world. During these years, I was so mean to Mama and told her often to shut up about the man who refused to see us. She kept retelling the same old stories about Papa, even though I hurled insult after insult at her with my abusive tongue. This was her way of keeping his memory alive during this long, rough period.

Junior high is a clumsy time for all students, but for me, all of the changes both physical and mental were excruciating.

I did branch out in junior high and included more people than my family in my life. But I still only allowed Mexicans to get close to me. Our church dominated our social life. Mama received solace from her faith; I enjoyed the social side of church. I loved the church dances. I was a good dancer, thanks to Papa.

The dances reminded me so much of Papa, though. He was an energetic dancer. When we lived in our homestead, we attended many dances in the area. Papa and Mama let out a holler when the three-piece band played their favorite song. They would dash out and dance around the campfire.

I loved the sound of the fiddle and the two guitars. We were lucky to have talented neighbors who loved to play for our gatherings.

Many times, Papa would grab my hand and drag me out to dance. At first, I fought him, but then he gave me private lessons at home, so I became a good dancer, too. I looked forward to those times he would dance with me.

In junior high, I concentrated on my schoolwork more than anything. I had set my focus on becoming a well-educated woman. Mr. Riley continued to encourage my pursuit of education and rewarded me every school year with cash for A's. I saved that money to put towards my college education.

High school wasn't much better, nothing to celebrate. I didn't participated in any fun extracurricular activities. I had to go home each day after school to help Mama in Mr. Riley's house and do my homework. I wanted no distractions from my one goal, to excel at the English language.

I dated no one in high school. Several boys showed interest in me, but I had no interest in them. I was too busy to get distracted.

My Mexican friends saw me as driven, but they seemed to understand. No one else had to go through high school without his or her Papa. My teachers seemed to understand my focus too. Many of them provided extra help. They applauded my determination.

One of my English teachers, Mr. Teague, suggested I also concentrate on being literate in Spanish. He understood the power of knowing two languages, so I spent many hours reading and writing Spanish. On my own, I checked out Spanish books from the library and devoured them.

Mama enjoyed my newfound interest in Spanish. She feared that I would turn my back on my mother tongue with my focus on English. In fact, I had refused to speak Spanish with her during my junior high years. This new interest excited her. We decided to speak as much Spanish every day as possible, and that really helped.

In 1937 I graduated from Trinidad Catholic High School in the top 5% of the class and received an academic scholarship to go to Trinidad State Junior College. I went there because of convenience and its affordable cost. The scholarship covered most of my two years at Trinidad State. Mr. Riley continued to pay me for work I did at his house with Mama. Working with Mama helped heal our relationship. The scholarship and my work covered my expenses. It also kept me in Trinidad near Mama.

My high school graduation day came, but I so missed Papa. The day marked me as a success because of my academic achievements, but I looked out at the crowd and saw Mama sitting by herself. A lump caught in my throat and I had to turn and look away to stop the tears. She had an empty seat next to her, maybe on purpose, for my Papa. He missed it by one year.

The years had passed and then there was only eleven months. That last year crept by the slowest. Isn't that the way it is?

The last stretch went on and on, but finally five days were all that remained in the ten-year sentence that my family served. It was 1938. I realized that as the time drew to an end. Papa was not the only one who had served that sentence. Papa's family, Mama and I, we all served those long years even though we were not in prison. We were imprisoned by our lives without him.

## 13

The big day that I had been waiting ten long years for finally arrived, Papa's homecoming. We gathered at *Tio* Miguel's house for the big event. He left early this morning to go and pick up Papa. He asked Mama and me to go with him, but we knew that Papa would not like it, so we refused his offer. We had grown accustomed to Papa's decision, and we wanted to help with the set-up at *Tio's* house.

I rose early that morning to sit outside in Mr. Riley's yard, overlooking Simpson Rest, breathing deeper than I had for years. Taking care of his yard had become one of my special projects. I loved the dirt under my fingernails and the smell of manure when I fertilized. I relished the blooms and fragrance that issued from my flowers, showing all my hard work. Mr. Riley again knew what he was doing to help heal me.

When I returned to our casita to dress, Mama smiled at me through tears as she said the Rosary. She had donned a new dress, bought for this special occasion. I also had a new dress to wear; I wanted Papa to see a grown up Maria today.

I heard a soft knock at the door. Mr. Riley stood there all dressed up and smiling in celebration "Do you need a ride to Miguel's house?" he questioned and held the door open. He knew that we would walk otherwise. We laughed and joked the whole way to *Tio* Miguel's house. Papa's family and friends shouted their greetings to us. It was going to be a great day.

Mr. Riley moved to the back of the living room to sit, even though he was an important member of the party. After helping set-up the rooms, I sat down beside him and gave him a hug and a kiss. My tears were close to exploding, but I controlled them.

Before I could catch my breath, Pablo, Rosa, and their now three grown sons walked in the front door, looking a little out of place. Mama and I raced across the living room to greet them, wondering how they knew about Papa's release.

Pablo's tears flowed freely as he replied, "The

Mexican community's gossip line has spread it through all of Las Animas County. We had to be here for my best friend, mi amigo." Rosa and Mama hugged and sobbed. They moved to a corner of the living room to catch up on their lives.

Their boys were not boys any longer but handsome young men. We felt awkward trying to talk and connect after years of absence. But I appreciated their coming to Papa's homecoming and continued small talk until they decided to move to the refreshment table.

I returned to the couch where Mr. Riley was still seated and explained who the family was. As I fidgeted waiting for Uncle Miguel to bring Papa home, I traveled back in time. I felt the anguish of waiting for Papa to come home from his shopping trip to Trinidad ten years ago and compared the two times, now and then. Waiting is hard at any age.

The little eight-year-old girl in me felt all the same anxiety she had felt before, but this time the eighteen-year-old young lady tried to hide all those emotions from her relatives and friends. In our nervous waiting, faces stared at me, trying to understand what was going on inside the composed shell they saw. Whispers and pointed fingers increased the tension for us all, but I refused to let them know the turmoil that boiled inside.

As I dealt with my grief in my last two years of high school, I withdrew from Papa's family, silent and stoic. I was a mess of emotion alone with Mama! I became aloof, calloused and withdrawn from everyone except Mama. Our relatives and friends from Trinidad saw me as the bitter hostile girl who had hurled many angry words at them and especially at my Mama.

Ten years of waiting, hoping, praying, crying and hating welled up inside me. I anticipated the moment of release. I strained with every ounce of my being, listening for the car that would carry him home. I first heard the car drive up in the driveway and before anyone else could move, I dashed out the door and into his arms. I don't know when Mama joined us. *Tio* Miguel moved back to let us have our time with Papa.

The sobs and tears we shared shook our three bodies to our cores. Sweet words filled the air, but I don't recall one word. I do remember that all my pent up anger towards Papa melted in his arms that day.

Again, I knew the loving embrace of my father. We celebrated for hours, as only Mexicans can. We danced, sang, drank and danced some more. Neither Mama nor I let Papa out of our sight for a single moment, feasting our eyes on him.

Throughout the whole day, I saw individual family members and friends hug Papa and talk to him. Often tears fell from both parties, but laughter exploded, too.

Papa's hair was gray and thinning. Wrinkles lined his face and the old familiar twinkle in his eyes had faded. The physical appearance of the man that had left me ten years ago was gone. Somehow he shrunk in size. He looked gaunt and defeated, but the spirit of the man had lived and grown. Papa was home!

After a late night of celebration, Mr. Riley drove Papa, Mama and me home. He placed Papa's small bag by the door and bid us *"Buenas Noches,"* a warm good night and closed the door softly behind him. We melted into the chairs at the kitchen table, holding hands and staring at each other. Papa repeated to me, "*Mi Hijita*! "My precious little daughter!" To Mama, he repeated, "*¡Mi Amor! ¡Mi preciosa!* "My love! My precious one!"

Our time to catch up had come; the words tumbled out of his mouth. He apologized for refusing to see us, but we assured him that he was forgiven. He refused to talk about his jail experience. Instead, he wanted me to fill in the last ten years for him. He asked about my schooling, my friends, living in Trinidad. He couldn't stop the questions. The one last question of the night was the one he had avoided all evening. What happened to our homestead east of Branson?

"We had to sell it, the cattle and our home. We were able to keep it for a couple years with Pablo and Rosa's help. A month after they took you, the sheriff came and took both horses. Papa, we tried! I tried so hard!" The words spilled out of my mouth in a heartfelt apology.

With tears streaming, Papa nodded his head with every statement I made. The answers soothed his aching heart. Mama and I cried with him and the moment was precious.

At dawn, we finally went to bed. Mama and Papa held hands as they said "*Buenas noches*," good night to me. I knew I couldn't sleep and that they needed some privacy, so I grabbed a sweater and went to Mr. Riley's garden, my sanctuary. The sunrise warmed my heart and the earth.

Everything was right--Papa was home!

## 14

I happily started a new chapter in my life, living with Papa and Mama together again. It always seemed so strange to see him in the city instead of out on the prairie, riding horses and being free. He looked peculiar without his cowboy hat, but he kept his boots. At first, he got a small part time job, working with his hands.

Due to the strenuous work and poor diet in jail, he had lost his physical strength, so Mama remained the main provider for a while. As soon as he regained his strength, he took on a full time job with Mr. Riley, and Mama quit hers. Mr. Riley let us stay in the casita, which had become our home. Papa and Mr. Riley became friends. Mr. Riley felt like he already knew Papa from all of our stories, and Papa so appreciated how Mr. Riley had taken care of me and provided work for Mama—and a home!

I treasure my last year at Trinidad State Junior College with Papa home. We valued any time we had together. We continued our weekly family gatherings at *Tio* Miguel's house after church. Now the time rang with more laughter and humor than ever before. So often before, when Papa was in jail, we talked of the injustice of his sentence. *Tio* Miguel tried it one time and Papa held his hand up and stopped him, saying, "No, we do not talk of such things."

Often Papa and I took walks into the hills above Trinidad near Simpson's Rest at dusk to look for wildlife. Those silent times with Papa were some of my favorite times in Trinidad because they reminded me of our time on the prairie. I think Papa felt the same way. At times we would see a buck or a porcupine, but the wildlife wasn't as plentiful as it had been on our homestead.

Papa tried to adjust to being out of jail, but he could not forget that he was a convict and felt shame. He spoke little of his jail years to anyone. But at times, he would get this far away look in his eyes and mutter to himself. We all knew he was going over those lost ten years, trying to understand the injustice of it all.

I had trouble understanding Papa's lack of hatred for what happened to him. His major feeling was shame; hatred was mine. As I watched him and how he reacted, I replaced impatience with him for the satisfaction of him being home. He frustrated me often with his passive manner. I felt he needed to be more assertive with *gringos*, but he didn't.

Trinidad State Junior College was a stepping-stone for me. After Trinidad, I had plans to go to Colorado State University in Fort Collins to get my bachelors' degree.

At the junior college, I had many long conversations with my career counselor about my future. My concentration on English and Spanish headed me into International Business. I planned to figure out the business world so I could make a success of myself. Two languages would give me a decisive edge.

After I graduated from Trinidad State Junior College, I moved four hours north to Fort Collins to attend Colorado State University. I received an academic scholarship that paid for most of my B.A. in International Business. My trips home to visit Papa and Mama became fewer and fewer as I became more involved in the university life.

There I sought out mostly Mexicans and found an informal group of students who felt like I did about our situation in the United States. Native Americans also joined this group. In this group I met an activist on campus and we married after a short courtship.

The basis for our attraction was our hatred, me for the *gringos* who had put an innocent Mexican man in jail for ten long years. My husband had experienced a similar family situation with prejudice. His family had homesteaded in the Taos, New Mexico area and lost their place because of similar language barriers and false accusations. His hatred of white people fed mine for the years we were together.

This hatred almost consumed me, rekindling the feelings that I had about my father's unfair jail sentence. During my marriage, I pulled away from my parents even though I was happy to have my Papa back and it should have been a wonderful time. Neither of my parents could understand the militant hatred my husband and I had or my absence.

Even though white people had wronged my dad, he didn't feel there was anything to do about it and harbored no hatred towards them. His best advice was to just forget it and move on—to better yourself. "*Olvídalo, mi hijita*." He said he could not live with the hatred I had, but that didn't work for me. I couldn't understand his complacency.

I saw that same attitude among his generation of Mexican-Americans in the Trinidad area; they did not want to fight the system. They wanted a peaceful life, leaving the *gringos* alone as much as possible. That's how they handled the situation, but I couldn't do it that way.

After graduating from C. S. U., we moved to Denver and I got a well-paying job as a business consultant for an International company. We had three children, two of them while we were attending C. S. U. My oldest son, Steven, was born in 1940 and then, Tom, my middle son in 1941. Our third child, Gabriela was born in 1942. I finally had the daughter I had always wanted. I hoped that we could salvage our marriage, so we tried to work things out for one more year, but it didn't work. In 1943, we divorced four years into our marriage.

Our compatibility changed when I landed a fulfilling job associating with many people from all over the world. This exposure changed my attitude.

After my divorce, my racial attitude continued changing. I realized that my husband's hatred had fueled mine. With him gone, the feelings disappeared. My worldview grew along with my new respect for my colleagues and neighbors, no matter what race they were.

After a few years of living in Trinidad near Papa's family and working for Mr. Riley, Papa and Mama missed me and my children too much, so it took little coaxing to convince them to move in with me in Denver. I had the pleasure of taking care of them in their old age. I went back to school and received a Masters in International Business in 1948. They helped out with my children while I went to school. The arrangement worked out well; the times were good.

Stories of our homestead life resurfaced, and Papa said to me in private often, "Let's take a trip back there!" But living in Denver was hard for my parents and me. I worked and traveled for my job; they cared for my children when I was gone. I appreciated their help, but I could see an emptiness in Papa's demeanor. He did not like living in Denver.

We spent much time talking about our homestead, east of Branson. My children enjoyed the after-dinner stories of the plains and horseback riding and begged their grandparents to repeat them.

Each time Papa retold a story, in my mind and soul I moved from the fast pace life of Denver to our peaceful home on the prairie. Time had healed my memories; now I remembered the good times on the plains, not just that single night.

The children enjoyed the stories but could not visualize the rock and adobe house that was our home and our life. It was so different from Denver and their lifestyle. Many times I would catch one of them staring at me and I knew they were trying to see me as that little cowgirl on the plains.

No one could look at me today in my three-piece business suit and heels and realize my humble country up bringing, even my own children. During one of our many nightly discussions after dinner, they asked what appeared to me silly, repetitive questions about what our house was like. "Now, where was the bathroom again? You didn't have indoor plumbing? You only had a two-room house? Where did you sleep, Mom? What is an outhouse?"

Because this conversation happened often, I finally suggested, "Well, what we need is a trip to Branson to see the house and the old homestead. What do you think?"

Wide eyes! "Yes, yes, yes," they screamed! Eager to join us, my children agreed to go but immediately realized they couldn't fit it into their busy schedules. There were track, baseball, and dance lessons. Wait, spring break was coming. We all could go then.

Papa's eyes twinkled with a new joy. Mama worried about the distance of the drive because Papa's health had been failing, but I would not take "No" for an answer, and he wasn't saying "No" anyway. He wanted to go! The children wanted to go too, but Mama didn't! Mama decided to stay at home. She had no real desire to see the homestead again. She couldn't forget that horrible night.

Papa begged Mama, but she was stubborn. The conversation drug on for days, but she never changed her mind.

## 15

It was 1953—thirty years since we moved to southeastern Colorado and our homestead. Now, I was thirty-three years old. Neither Papa nor I had been back to the homestead—me since we sold it and Papa since he went to jail.

Before we left Denver, I called Mr. Horner to make sure it would be OK for us to go out to the "Philly Place." His son, Harold, had taken over for him and said it would be fine. In fact, he was anxious to meet Papa and me. I wondered if he knew the story of my Papa.

Papa and I packed up the car with my three children and drove the 250 miles to our former home. Steven, Tom and Gabriela were in for a treat!

The trip was delightful. We left Denver at 7:00

am; Papa wanted to get an early start. We stopped in Trinidad and visited family we had not seen for years. My children met *Tio* Miguel and his family for the first time, and they hit it off. Tom, my middle son, looked and sounded like his uncle. We didn't stay long though because Papa was anxious to get to Branson. He had not seen the house for twenty-five years.

While we lived in Trinidad, he couldn't go back to the place because it had been a part of his parole agreement not to return to the old homestead. That agreement had expired many years ago, so now he was free to return. With our busy lives, this opportunity had never come up before—it was time.

The trip from Trinidad to Branson flew by, one hour packed full of reminiscing. When we got to Branson, we stopped at Mr. Horner's house, and he directed us to his son, Harold's house. Harold met us at the front door with a friendly handshake and invitation inside his house. We asked permission to go out to the old homestead. Harold had taken over for his father and allowed us on his property.

He seemed glad to meet us. Maybe he wondered about the horse thief story that he had heard his whole life. He was polite and asked no questions. In fact, he seemed delighted that we wanted to see the old Philly Place. Harold introduced us to his wife, Elva, and she hugged each one of us. She especially made over my three children. My daughter, Gabriela, snuggled up with her on the sofa and enjoyed Elva's affection. The boys endured her hugs but I heard them say later that they liked Elva and her hugs.

Having to ask permission to visit our home appeared so strange to me because it still seemed like it belonged to us. As we headed the car east out of Branson on the dirt road, I glanced over at Papa. Tears streamed down his cheeks; I joined him. My children respected our pain and kept quiet, for a change. In the rearview mirror, I saw each of them wipe a tear or two. They truly did understand.

"My heart has always been here, *mi hijita*. Even though Mexico is my home country, this land took my heart. Many long nights I laid awake in jail remembering this land, its sounds and smells, the wind, the dust, the peacefulness. I redrew each acre of our homestead and remembered all the good times we had here. This is home and always will be!"

As he finished this statement, something deep within me shifted and agreed with him. No matter where I live, this will always be home, and I finally realized this. As we turned off the main dirt road down a dusty old path, I felt the excitement mount; we were almost there.

It was only a couple miles to our homestead. We headed southeast towards the mesa, parallel to a fence line. The mesa had been our backdrop and stood in front of us now. The wide-open prairie was all around us on three sides. This all felt so familiar. I strained to see our house.

I wondered if our house was still standing or just a pile of rubbish. We topped a small hill and my heart jumped within me. My eyes scanned the horizon. The reservoir to the east glistened in the sunshine. It was full because of an abundant summer rainfall. The arroyo in front of our house reminded me of so many peaceful mornings and nights with Papa watching for wildlife. The gramma grass was green and tall, waving in the breeze. A herd of antelope raced across our path and dove under the fence, running east to some unknown destination. That scene echoed through my mind back to those years here.

The drastic change caught me off guard. Years of erosion and vacancy had taken its toll on the house, but the stone walls still stood solid. Some of the adobe mortar still held the rocks in place. We sped down that dusty road as fast as we could. When we stopped in a cloud of dust, we sat for several minutes in the car staring at our home.

## 16

With quiet reverence, we got out of the car and walked toward the front of our house. Our beautiful front door was gone—no hint of the blue paint we loved. No furniture remained in the main room that had served as our kitchen, living room and my bedroom, because we took all we had to Trinidad when we moved.

But in the corner of my parent's bedroom was the fainting couch that Papa had bought Mama many years ago. Now it was rusty and ragged, with only a couple spots of material still attached, a skeleton of the beautiful extravagant piece of furniture that it once had been.

"¿*Por qué*? Why did she leave it, Maria? That was the only special gift I had ever given her. It meant so much to her and to me. Why?" Dumbfounded, Papa cried.

Tears ran down his cheeks and he doubled over with a sob, grabbing the edge of the fainting couch to steady himself. The pained look on Papa's face scared me, reminding me of his fragile health and age.

"Papa, at first she sat glued to her it all day long. She would run her fingers over the wooden trim and cry and cry, repeating your name. She only got up to go the bathroom and go to bed, but many mornings I would go in to wake her up, and she was sleeping on the fainting couch.

She did finally stop sleeping on it, but I often found her seated there, hands clasped in front of herself, crying.

She could not take it with her. It represented something so special that you had shared; she could not bear even to look at it. I think it reminded her of the absurdity of our situation. She knew you were a good man and that couch represented that goodness to her; so she just left it here. It was less painful that way. Otherwise, it would have been a constant reminder of that horrible night.

The day we moved out of this house, I knew her heart was breaking when she told Pablo to leave the fainting couch in the bedroom, but we didn't talk about it then, because there was so much going on anyway. We both spent the whole day crying and had it not been for Pablo and other friends, I don't know how we would have moved.

Neither Mama nor I packed a single thing; our friends did it all. Mama and I sat out on the edge of the arroyo, looking out over this vast land and holding each other, as one against the world. When they had Pablo's wagon packed, we jumped on the back and never looked back because our hearts were breaking for the second time. One day in our conversation, she told me exactly what I've told you today about the fainting couch."

As I completed this explanation, I hoped it would help ease his pain. And by the look on his face, it must have done the job. After settling that, we studied every inch of that house, recalling with joy our lives shared there. I saw the exact place in the adobe wall where I turned to every night and studied it until I fell asleep. Some of the straw patterns still showed. We looked out the space where the windows used to be at the familiar view we had seen so many times.

Papa started each statement off with "Maria, remember when, *recuerdo cuando. . .*" He had learned

English and spoke impeccably, but back here in his old familiar surroundings, the Spanish language came naturally and I loved hearing those precious sounds. Neither one of us wanted to stop our examining and the memories. The stories were endless and being here where they actually happened made them all alive and real. It didn't matter that most of the roof had rotted--there were only two *vigas* still attached but the ladrillas were all gone. Three gaping holes stood where the windows had been. Our blue door vanished. We had shared our lives here; this was home!

My children tried to listen to my painstaking tour of the house with Papa for a little while, but they wanted to explore outside. They ran around the house, finding all kinds of treasures strewn around the house and where the corral had been. One would come to me and grab my hand, dragging me out the door, saying, "Momma, what's this? Was this Papa's? Was this yours?" It was a treasure hunt for them.

Outside, I gathered them around me and showed them where the corral had been. I took them down to the arroyo where Papa and I did our morning and nightly vigil of animal watching. I pointed out certain places on the land that had meaning to Papa and me. They couldn't get over how big it was and how far it was from anyone else.

Papa followed behind us and laughed when a memory struck a chord with him.

"What is this, Maria?" Papa rushed passed me to a piece I had completely forgotten.

"Our wagon, *nuestro carro*, Papa!" I joined him, as we looked at a rusted mess of wood and metal.

"Why did you leave it here?" he asked with disbelief etched on his face. No self-respecting rancher could live without a wagon.

"They took the horses, remember, *recuerdos*? I borrowed Pablo's horses when we lived here. How could we take it to Trinidad without horses?"

His silence answered me.

We headed back to the house, enjoying the sound of my children running and laughing in circles around us. Their sheer joy helped erase the reminder of what we lost with our wagon.

I scoured the area with Papa, seeing rusted and worn relics, scattered here and there. We squealed when we found different items: a broken crock lid, a chip of a blue glass, and farming equipment to plow the field. I encouraged each of my children to select one small souvenir to take home.

## 17

W e continued circling the house to see what we could see. My adventurous middle son, Tom, had wandered off farther away than anyone else. Noticing his absence, I hollered for him to come back because I wanted to leave soon.

I heard his voice and moved around to the back of the house, looking south towards the mesa. I started towards him, but he hustled towards me after my second shout. He had the bottom of his t-shirt drawn up like a bowl and carried something in it. He had trouble walking and carrying his treasure without tripping. What had he found up in the trees that dotted the mesa?

"What are these things? Can we eat them?" Tom

demanded because he knew I was the expert. He held up a small brown nut between two fingers.

"*Piñones!*" I squealed.

Papa, Steven and Gabriela caught up with us sooner than I would expect Papa capable to do. He was breathless, but his curiosity about what Tom had found forced him to scurry along with the other two.

Papa chuckled. After catching his breath, he said, "*Recuerdo cuando. . .* Remember when we learned about *piñones*. We had never picked them before, but Papa had brought a small bag home with him on one of his trips to Trinidad the last fall we were together. Those nuts had been left over from the last big harvest and Papa didn't have to pay much for them. Even though they were old, we loved their flavor.

We went with Pablo, Rosa and their boys picking up *piñones* on the mesa here behind our house. We were told that you only see a sizable crop of *piñones* every seven years or so. We knew we needed to harvest as many as we could because we could make some extra money selling them in Branson. Also, we all loved the flavor of *piñones* as a treat on a cold, dark winter night by the fireplace.

We took an old blanket with us and Pablo's

middle son shimmied up the tree. Holding onto the branch above his head, he jumped on the lower branches. It rained *piñones* down on our blanket. What fun! What an easy task this was! Really!

We spent the afternoon down on our hands and knees and gathered these precious gems and put them into a gunny sack, hoping to fill it up.

Some *piñon* cones fell down too and no one had warned us about the sap on the cones. Each of us became a sticky mess pulling the *piñones* out of the cones. The *piñones* stuck to the cones, to the blanket and to us.

We learned our lesson that day about sap. It took us months to get the gooey mess off of our fingers.

We continued our *piñon* picking for the rest of the afternoon, and we filled two gunny sacks—one for us and one for Pablo's family. When we got home, Rosa and Mama roasted the *piñones* and we shared a nice dinner with Pablo's family. The next time we went to Branson, we sold all we had to the people there in no time. We did keep some for ourselves."

Papa added this funny part to the story telling, "The next morning after harvesting the *piñones*, I screamed when I rolled out of bed. My butt was so sore from being down on my knees, scrunched up all afternoon. Mama was the second to chime in with her pain. Maria, remember, *recuerdo*, you didn't want to admit how sore you were, but I saw you hobbling around the house to the corral and chuckled to myself.

Some friends told us about making coffee out of the roasted *piñon* nuts, so we tried that. Boy was that tasty!"

Papa finally took a deep breath and ended his tale. This long forgotten story of our first *piñon* picking experience delighted me anew. Papa's description of that little nut and our first experience brought it all back to life.

I examined Tom's fingers and didn't find any sap. He had gathered the *piñones* from off of the ground so he was safe.

The five of us walked up to the *piñon* trees along the slope of the mesa and picked up as many as we could handle off the ground. Steven volunteered to run back to the car to get a paper grocery bag from the trunk. The children filled it up before we left.

Steven's eager interest in the *piñones* tickled me because he is my more reserved son and usually does not want to participate in anything we do. Gabriela and Tom are always ready to jump in for the adventure, but not Steven. How exciting to see him ready to take part here, of all places.

As I watched them move so deftly at picking up the *piñones*, I watched my elderly Papa move slowly and with caution. He couldn't bend over and reach the ground so the youngsters suggested he hold the bag and they would come to him. The small size of the *piñones* was a problem, too—he's not seeing as clearly. On his last visit to the ophthalmologist, we learned he has a cataract on his left eye that needs attention in the next couple months. So many of those precious little nuts escape my Papa's eyes.

I stood back and watched the scene unfolding before me. I saw three generations enjoying our homestead, nature, and our home! I had to turn around and wipe a tear—a tear of joy this time, instead of sorrow!

Over the years, I remembered seeing *piñones* for sale by vendors along the road when we lived in Trinidad, but we never bought any. At various times I had a vague memory of something to do with *piñones,* but I had never recalled this specific delightful *piñon* incident. In fact, I would get an uneasy feeling when I saw *piñon* sellers, but I didn't know why.

We never bought any because we couldn't afford

them. They were so expensive, and I loved their flavor, but something wouldn't even let me think of buying them.

Today I understand the feeling—again, it had been the connection with the loss of my Papa, our homestead and the good times there.

The time to leave had come, but I hated to end this precious time we had shared.

"Kids, Papa, we need to go. One last look at the house and then we are leaving," I announced with a deep sadness in my voice.

It took a few minutes to round up my children. Tom wanted to get the last *piñones* he could. Steven sat by the edge of the arroyo looking northeast. Gabriela held Papa's hand and quizzed him about something very important to her.

They kept saying, "One more, Mama, one more!"

Papa let go of Gabriela's hand and turned his back to me and gazed at the mesa, lost in his memories. I had to prod him along the most. Leaving a place you love is hard!

To break the spell this place had on him, I shouted, "Let's go! ¡*Vámonos*!

## 18

I returned to the house for one last look inside. Papa joined me. As we were leaving the house and our past, something caught my eye in the dirt by the front step. Wondering what this strange object was at my feet, I bent over and using my manicured nails pried free a blue marble.

At first, it meant nothing to me. I rolled it around in my smooth hand, fingers gliding over it. To whom could it belong? Why was it still here? Then I suddenly realized whose it was. "Papa, Papa, my blue marble! I found my blue marble!"

I screamed and tears came without warning. It all came back to me in a flash.

"The night they took you away, I destroyed my doll and tossed all my marbles out the door. I guess losing those dear things represented losing my Papa, maybe like Mama leaving her fainting couch. Oh, Papa, this blue marble was the treasure of my childhood. Remember, you took me to Trinidad, taught me to play marbles, and I beat every child in *Tio* Miguel's neighborhood."

The joy that I felt in finding that lost blue marble is beyond words. I still have that marble today as a treasure in my jewelry box at home and running across that marble started the retelling of this story and remembering once again.

Finding that marble that day seemed to quiet a part of me that had been restless and disturbed since childhood--no, since that one life-changing night! I shoved it deep in my pocket to make sure I wouldn't lose it again. After walking back to the corrals and all around the house one last time, we finished the day with pictures.

Steven took pictures of Papa and me and the house. I took pictures of my children with Papa in front of our house. Papa took a picture of my children and me in the doorway. We knew Mama would want to see them and I planned to frame them all.

I blushed as I asked Steven to take a picture of my blue marble, and he eagerly smiled, saying, "Oh, Momma, I would love to take a picture of you with your trophy. Maybe you will teach us how to play marbles." I nodded my head as I turned and wiped a tear from my eyes—I hadn't played marble in years.

It was hard to leave, but we both felt good about the experience. For both of us, peace had replaced the despair and anguish of many hard years. For my children, they now could see where I grew up and understand the setting of our stories.

With reluctance, we walked back to the car. My children piled into the back seat, grabbing for water and books to read on the trip home. Before I knew what happened, Papa stopped in his tracks, turned on his heels and disappeared back inside the house.

I waited wondering. He reappeared dragging behind him the fainting couch. With a sheepish grin on his face, he questioned me, "Can we take this home for Mama? Please? *¿Por favor?*"

My heart melted because I realized he wanted Mama to share in this beautiful visit to the past that we had experienced and this was how she could join us.

My answer to his question was silence. I flipped the trunk open and we maneuvered this valuable treasure in sideways after moving our suitcases around. Our trip back to Branson was quiet! We stopped and thank Harold and Elva. He asked how we found the place. We shared our joy with him.

I decided to tell him about taking the old fainting couch. He chuckled and said, "When we have visited the old Philly Place, I have often wondered about that couch. It just didn't seem to fit into a rock and adobe homestead house. Thanks for the explanation." He encircled Elva in his arms as he thanked us, and I saw in their eyes a deep understanding of our taking that old piece of junk.

Harold seemed really pleased and invited us back to visit anytime we wanted. His wife wanted a picture of us all to share with people in the community. She kept saying that she knew people would remember us. She offered us homemade pecan pie and tea. We cut the visit short because I knew Papa wanted to recapture the whole experience with Miguel and his family, and it was getting late.

We stopped in Trinidad for the night and recounted the whole day to *Tio* Miguel and his family. During our dinner, each of us would break into a litany of "You should have seen . . ." Miguel and his family delighted in our joy and listened to stories for hours. What I enjoyed was the stories my children told—they really got into the whole experience. It was a late night.

Tom told about our piñon adventure and offered to share our treasures. He described the excursion with lots of specifics—I was so proud of what he remembered.

Steven agreed that he liked the piñon picking, but he also told *Tio* Miguel that he would send him copies of the pictures he took out on the homestead. He listed all the pictures he took and emphasized my picture with the marble. How precious that was!

Gabriela chimed in about her enjoyment at the homestead and how she so enjoyed my stories about the place. She also told how much she liked Elva's hug. I knew that she had enjoyed them, but this surprised me.

As I went to sleep that night, I felt a peace and calm I hadn't felt in years. This trip home had truly healed me in ways I didn't understand. I turned to the wall in *Tio* Miguel's house and I drifted off to sleep remembering the straw patterns in the adobe mortar in our homestead house. I dreamed of wind, horses, wildlife, the open prairie and purple mesas.

Papa was up at 6:00 am and woke the children and me. We had a quick breakfast and said our good-byes to *Tio* Miguel. We promised to come back soon. I saw tears in Miguel's eyes as we left.

We drove to Denver with minimal conversation, Papa deep in thought and me, too. Upon our arrival, Papa jumped out of the car like a teenager, grabbed the old fainting couch and propped it up by the car. Looking through the front window, I saw Mama's face.

She dashed out the front door and cried, "How did you know that I have wondered about that beautiful couch for years? I never said anything to you because you had never mentioned its absence. That was so hard for me to leave that couch the day we moved, but I couldn't bear to take it out of our bedroom to my lonely room in Trinidad without you. I hope you understand that."

Papa did understand and he placed that old, rusty fainting couch in the corner of their bedroom in my house. The three of us enjoyed its presence. My children talked like they had a hard time understanding its value, but I saw each of them bring a friend by to see it. Somehow the trip made a difference for us all--Papa and I had healed wounds.

Mama had her fainting couch. I had my blue marble, and my children had stories to tell to their friends. Each of them had brought back a memento of this wonderful experience and found a place of honor to put them which surprised me.

I saw Tom go to the trunk and rummaged through the suitcases and souvenirs from our trip. He found what he was looking for and handed the bag of *piñones* we had picked to my mother and said, "Grandma, can you roast these for us?"

Mama squealed with delight, "I haven't had *piñones* since we picked them so many years ago. Yes, I will for sure!"

Papa smiled with the old twinkle; his walk had a new bounce. The hatred in my heart had completely melted. I had reconciled many details that had ruined my life, and I had that small blue marble to remind me. This trip back into the past became important to Papa and me because he died six months later.

Often in his last months, he would visibly leave us and return in his mind to the high dry prairie that he loved, riding Rusty and doing the work he loved. A serene smile curved his lips and he was at peace with the world, but his serenity ended as he neared the end.

His dying words to Mama and me tear at my heart, even today, because once again the peace is gone, and uncertainty and anger exist. I had conveniently forgotten those demanding words until I found that blue marble today, and it brought it all back! The joy, the sorrow, the peace, and the hatred!

Papa left me with a mission that I will spend the rest of my life trying to complete, "*Mi hijita, mi esposa preciosa*, I love you, *te amo*, and I always have and always will. I hope that you are not ashamed of me for being a convict, but you must know something before I die. I never shared the horror of the jail time for me. Also, I never shared the pain, the anguish I faced that fateful night!"

Mama and I both drew closer, curious about this man's secret. He labored for a breath. We did not want to miss one word. His voice weakened with life leaving him, but he said this next sentence with his last strength and clarity, looking me straight in the eyes, "I did not steal any horses. Maria, you know that. You must prove that fact so that you can clear my name--your name. You must prove my innocence."

And with those words and that charge, Papa died in the spring of 1954. And that has become my mission, to clear the name of a good Mexican man.

"Oh, Papa, don't die! Don't leave me! I love you! *¡Ayudame mi Dios!*" My life's job was set by that simple sentence, to clear a good man's name and I will!

## PHOTO ALBUM

In September, 2015, my brother, Harold, and I visited the Philly Place which is now on the Doherty ranch. We hadn't been there for about twenty years.

Here are some pictures we took from that sight-seeing trip. Some of the treasures we found ended up in this story.

*The Philly Homestead as it is today. Notice the vigas that remain on the roof.*

*Looking south from the arroyo up to the homestead*

*The wagon we found near the homestead that is referenced in the story*

*The back of the homestead looking north and east towards Mesa de Mayo*

*Meet one of Paco's relatives, a horny toad.*

*Paco, the horny toad*

# MAP OF COLORADO

## REVIEW MY BOOK PLEASE

If you enjoyed this historical fiction about southeastern Colorado during a time of homesteading and heartache for this Mexican immigrant family, please go to Amazon and review it for me!

When Will Papa Get Home?

## CURRENT PROJECTS

- *A Time To Grow Up—A Daughter's Grief Memoir,* a grief memoir in poetry and prose about my Dad and Mom's death. To be released June 2017
- *Marshall Flippo* - biography of the legendary square dance caller
- *Eyewitness to Life* - a woman's fiction
- And one more Tumbleweed book—more poems & stories about growing up in Branson, CO! There are so many!

# ABOUT THE AUTHOR

Larada Horner-Miller is an emerging author of historical fiction. This is Larada's second book.

She gained a BA in English, with a minor in Spanish and a concentration in education, and a MEd in integrating technology in the curriculum. She is now retired after a twenty-seven-year career teaching middle school.

She co-owns and manages a ranch in southeastern Colorado with her brother. "The Philly Place" now is on her aunt's ranch. Her imagination was sparked after she found a marble while exploring this old homestead on her family's original ranch.

She is the author of *This Tumbleweed Landed*; *From Grannie's Kitchen Cookbook, Volume 1*; and *Let Me Tell You a Story*, and the coauthor of *Branson-Trinchera Historic Photos* with Tom Cummins and *Building Capacity with the Common Core State Standards for ELA-Literacy* with Karen White.

She and her husband Lin live in the mountains

above Albuquerque, New Mexico, near the village of Tijeras. She enjoys dancing, traveling, knitting, and reading.

larada.wix.com/author

larada@earthlink.net

## EXCERPT FROM NEW BOOK

The following poem is an excerpt from *A Time to Grow Up—A Daughter's Grief Memoir* also by Larada Horner-Miller (Paperback & eBook, $19.95, ISBN: 0996614427).

Snuggle into the Memories

Written on: March 20, 2014

> *I lost Mom,*
> *about 1 year ago!*
> *Today I sit in her house*
> *surrounded by her*
> *and*
> *snuggled into the memories!*

*No, no longer fighting the loss,*
*not running away*
*from the memories!*

*But snuggle into them,*
*lay my head on her shoulder*
*like so many times before*
*breathe in her body fragrance*
*like so many times before*
*laugh with her—her blue eyes dancing*
*like so many times before*
*dance with her trying to recapture*
*Dad's special step*
*like so many times before.*

*Memories comfort me*
*today!*
*Hundreds of precious moments*
*shared.*

*I lean into them.*
*They brush my cheek*
*kiss my brow*
*caress my shoulder*
*live deep in my heart!*

*I can't bring her back!*
*I tried,*
*and it doesn't work!*
*I can't go with her,*
*not yet!*

*So today*
*I snuggle into the memories.*
*I speak her name.*
*I speak her joy.*
*I speak her laughter.*
*I speak her fears.*
*I speak her faith.*

*I speak Mom!*

www.ingramcontent.com/pod-product-compliance
Lightning Source LLC
Chambersburg PA
CBHW052144170626
46812CB00004B/1583